Promising Meg

by Anna Huckabee

ISBN: 9781794429932

To my sister Joanna,

who read this book when it was painfully bad and still told me it was one of the most romantic books she'd ever read.

I love you, girl!

Chapter One

Amiens, France, August 1918

The hair under Jack's metal helmet was the only dry place on him. The rest of him was soaked to the bone. The infernal rain hadn't let up for days and showed no sign of stopping. The only good thing about the rain was it gave him a chance to wash off the mud.

The mud. They slogged through it day and night. It clung to their boots, their clothes, their skin. They couldn't lie down to sleep because of it. If they tried to sleep sitting up and leaning against the side of the trench, they'd slide right down the muddy wall.

Jack shivered inside his heavy coat and longed for a fire. If he had a fire, he'd risk pneumonia and take his shoes off to get his socks dry. If he had a fire, he'd make a decent pot of coffee. Hot coffee. He'd find a way to heat the tins of food from their rations. Hot food. Oh, the agony contained in the mere thought of it.

At least there wasn't a breeze in the trench. The trench got pretty miserable in the heat of the sun, with no place to go for shade. But in this incessant rain, the lack of a breeze was a blessing, possibly the only thing standing between him and hypothermia.

The lieutenant walked up the narrow passage and all the soldiers snapped to attention. A bullet from the enemy trench pinged into the dirt piled on the far side of their trench just over the top of Cavanaugh's head. All the men ducked.

Jack glanced at Cavanaugh. The soldier gripped his metal helmet and crouched his tall, lanky form into the hole even further.

1

"You okay?" Jack hissed.

"Yeah. Missed me by that much." Cavanaugh held his fingers up to show the distance.

"Whatever you do, stay down," Lieutenant Stafford said as he made his way past the men. He didn't stop when he reached Jack. "Walk with me."

Jack fell into step behind his commanding officer. They slipped and slid their way to the small cave dug out of the dirt mound that served as a command center for their unit. Jack straightened to his full height once he was safe inside the tiny room. He wiped the moisture off his face with his hand. His hand came away muddy.

"I'd offer you a handkerchief but none of mine are clean," said the lieutenant.

The two men smirked at each other at the running joke. Then the lieutenant grew somber.

"Orders came from headquarters. We're to assist taking the town beyond that hill."

Jack became aware of the artillery fire he could hear the distance. He'd grown so accustomed to its presence that he barely noticed it anymore. "When, sir?"

"Under cover of darkness tomorrow morning. They've been battering away at them. We're to make a run for it when we hear the artillery start up down here. We'll meet up with the rest of the brigade as soon as we clear the enemy trench."

Jack's stomach clenched with a combination of fear and excitement. They'd finally be getting out of this mud pit and doing the job they'd come to do.

"I'll need you to help prepare the men, Sergeant Collins. Hopefully, we don't have to come back here. They'll need to take as many provisions as they can carry in their packs and still fight." The lieutenant stopped pacing and stared into the distance. "Just think, if we take the town, we could sleep under cover tonight, out of the rain. We might be able to have a fire."

The hope of a fire pushed the fear into the background. Jack's imagination returned to his earlier daydream. Hot coffee. Hot food. Dry clothes. He'd be willing to try just about anything to get it.

The lieutenant slapped him on the shoulder. "I'll let you get to it, then. Inform the men. Good luck."

∞

The darkness had never seemed this intense to Jack back home in Indiana. The eery glow of something burning in the distance cast bizarre shadows on the mound of dirt above them. Inside the trench, the men couldn't see their hands in front of their faces. At least it had stopped raining. Tomorrow would probably be hot and humid.

Jack could make out the dim form of the lieutenant on the embankment in front of them. Cavanaugh stood behind him, waiting to head up and out.

Suddenly, the sky lit with flames and the air exploded with mortars detonating.

"That's the signal," the lieutenant called in a low voice.

As one, the men surged up the embankment and out of the trench. Crouched, they sprinted across the field toward the enemy.

A high pitched whine filled the air. "Incoming!" someone yelled before the earth shook with an explosion that threw the field into sharp relief.

Men charged forward, bayonets fixed, shooting at the men swarming over the lip of the trench in front of them.

Time slowed to a crawl. Jack fired, reloaded, fired again. He couldn't tell if he was hitting anything in this strange light. He could see the network of enemy trenches in front of him, could hear the cries of the enemy soldiers. Then a word he understood pierced through his consciousness.

"Gas!"

Jack dropped to his knees. He fumbled with the strap attached to his gas mask and yanked it loose, then pulled it over his face. He couldn't see well through the lenses. He stumbled back to his feet and, crouching, made his way forward once more.

A scream to his left jerked his attention from the goal. A man lay writhing on the ground. Blood spread from a wound on his leg.

Cavanaugh.

Jack turned and stumbled toward his friend. The tall man gripped his leg, his gun forgotten on the ground beside him.

"Come on, man, we have to get you back to our side and get you patched up." Jack scooped the bigger man under the arms and hefted him to his feet. With one arm over his shoulders, he half dragged, half carried Cavanaugh back the way they'd come.

"Fall back!" came the cry in the distance.

Jack's heart fell. Their mission tonight had been a failure. If Cavanaugh died, it would have been in vain.

The two men stumbled down the slope into the trench. Jack fell to his knees next to his friend and tried to see what was wrong with his leg. The fires lighting the night sky provided a harsh view of the blood spreading down Cavanaugh's pant leg.

Jack ripped the cloth and tore off a long strip. He wrapped it around Cavanaugh's leg and tied it as tight as he could.

Cavanaugh clutched at his arm. "You have to tell her," he gasped.

"Tell who?" Jack asked, puzzled.

"Tell her I loved her. Tell her I thought of her day and night. Tell her..." The man's voice faded and his eyes glassed over. One last breath escaped his lungs and he sagged back onto the muddy ground.

"No!" Jack screamed. "No! You have to tell her yourself!"

The eery light revealed something white resting against Cavanaugh's chest. Jack wiped what blood he could off his hands onto Cavannaugh's pant leg, mixing the blood evenly with mud and rain. Then he gingerly picked up the paper.

A beautiful woman looked back at him. She held a tiny baby in a white dress. Cavanaugh's wife. He'd spoken of her often over the course of the last months. Jack tucked the picture into his damp coat pocket. Then he waited, still wearing the cumbersome gas mask.

When nothing happened, he dared a look over the edge of the trench. Bodies were strewn about the field. Here and there, fires burned where mortars had struck the damp earth, but these were sputtering.

Jack hauled himself back up over the edge of the trench and jogged across the field toward the distant town. Sounds of battle had moved away from his location and he followed the noise, even though it went against his better judgment.

That's when the odor assaulted his senses, the sulfuric scent of mustard gas. In the darkness and smoke from mortar fires, he couldn't see where it originated. He pressed on, moving ever closer to the town. Gunfire and screams pierced the night. Every instinct screamed to run away. Go back to Cavanaugh. That would be cowardly. He pressed forward.

At the outskirts of the town, he caught up with men from his brigade. They fought their way forward house by house, road by road, until they reached the far side.

Fires lit by the artillery barrage turned the night sky as light as day. They rose over an embankment of clouds that mingled with the smoke so one couldn't tell where the smoke ended and the clouds began. The light showed the backs of their enemy retreating in front of them.

The lieutenant appeared by Jack's side. "I see you found your way back to us," he said.

Jack pulled off his gas mask and reattached it to his pack. "Yes, sir."

"Where did you disappear to earlier?"

"Cavanaugh was hit. I took him back to the trench to try to help him. He didn't make it."

5

The lieutenant stared into the distance once more. His jaw clenched. Muscles in his face worked. His voice cracked when he finally spoke. "He was a good man."

Jack nodded his agreement. He didn't dare do more. He'd never get the words out.

∞

That night they slept in a barn near the road. The drenching rain poured onto the neglected roof, but only reached the floor where it leaked. The former owners of the farmland were long gone, likely forced out by the army that now retreated in front of them.

Jack stripped out of his wet coat, socks, and shirt, and hung them to dry over a loose board. They lit a fire and made coffee. They took turns heating small cans of provisions. They laughed, told stories. Jack observed the light spirits but didn't feel like joining them. He leaned against the barn wall and fingered the photo of Cavanaugh's wife and child. How would he break the news to them?

A colonel entered the barn and the men snapped to attention. He waved them to 'at ease', then gathered the commanding officers. Jack could just make out their conversation.

"We want to press the advantage here, but we can't get too far ahead of our supply lines."

"What about casualties?"

"What about reinforcements?"

"The mobile hospital is a day behind us. They'll be picking up the wounded, treating them, and sending them back behind the lines for care."

Jack looked back at the picture in his hand. They were too late for Cavanaugh.

∞

Jack woke before dawn the next morning. The rain had stopped in the night. His clothing was dry. He was warm. In fact, he was so warm, he felt like he was on fire. His legs were burning. Someone nearby was screaming. The realization slowly dawned that it was him. He was screaming. The pain was so unbearable he couldn't stop.

Strong hands gripped his shoulders and the lieutenant's face swam into focus.

"You have to get yourself together, man!" he shouted into Jack's face.

Jack could barely breath. He gasped in air and forced himself to let it out. That helped. He did it again. "My legs," he managed to croak out.

"You've been gassed. Must have happened in the battle last night."

Jack looked down and realized he wasn't wearing trousers. They'd been stripped off him and were burning in the cook fire.

"We had to get those off you so it didn't get worse," the lieutenant explained.

Jack nodded. He didn't want the trousers on in the first place. Blisters covered both legs. They seeped yellow fluid into a puddle on the ground. Someone came with clean water from the farm well and began to wash his legs. Jack writhed on the ground in agony, doing everything in his power to stifle the screams.

"Breathe!" came a command from somewhere above him.

Jack sucked in a lungful of air.

"Let it out!"

He forced it out with a 'whoosh'.

"Do that again!"

Breath by agonizing breath he got through the cleaning. Then he lay gasping and sweating on the barn floor.

"We don't have anything clean to wrap him with."

"Then leave it. It's better for it to be open than to be wrapped in dirty cloth."

"The ambulance will be here sometime today. They'll pick you up and take you back to the hospital," came the lieutenant's voice.

Jack nodded. "I can't quit now. We've finally gotten them on the run."

"Your fighting days are over, sergeant. You have served your country well. Now rest. You have a long road in front of you."

Chapter Two

Meg woke to a loud *thunk* and the grating metal on metal sound of a pot scraping across the stove in the kitchen below. She rolled toward the window in her room. Early morning light poured through the window and across the bed. Another pan scraped. Gran must be lighting the stove to make the morning coffee.

Meg dressed and went downstairs to the kitchen. Gran bent over the stove, putting the last touches on Sunday lunch and sliding it into the oven.

"The roast is ready for dinner," Gran said as she puttered about putting the matches back and replacing seasonings on the little shelf by the stove.

"Did Nellie or Aunt Elaine ever say what they're bringing?"

"Elaine told me she'd bring a dessert, maybe chocolate cake."

Sunday dinner was a family tradition. Meg looked forward to it every week. Uncle Daniel, Aunt Elaine, and their daughter, Nellie ate with them after church.

Meg enjoyed every moment of the walk to church on this glorious fall Sunday. For being in her eighties, Gran was still spry. As they made their way to church, Gran had no trouble keeping up with Meg and greeted everyone they met by name.

Meg loved fall. The chilly nights of September gave way to warm days. The leaves were beginning to change colors. The leaves

9

would be perfect this year, if the weather held. Sometimes a Nor'easter would come in and wash all of them away in its wind and vicious downpours. Meg always felt sorry for the trees when that happened. It was as if they'd been stripped out of their vibrant dresses and left cold, wet, and naked in the weather. She hoped this year they could keep their loveliness intact until true winter crept upon them and the snow could wrap them in its brilliant, white coat.

Meg watched those who were walking along with them to church. She saw families, children in line behind their parents, all dressed in their Sunday finery. Meg looked to see if the Grocer, Mr. Miller, had come with his wife and children. The rumor mill often turned with gossip about them. Mr. Miller was said to be an Atheist. Others said that he'd had an argument with Rev. Norton and refused to go to church ever again. Still others said that he was afraid to leave his store unattended even for the short time they were in church. Whatever the reason, as it happened every Sunday, Mrs. Miller and their 3 children exited the alley behind the store alone. Meg could see Mr. Miller peering between the slats on the store windows.

Hollis was a peaceful place, whatever Mr. Miller might think. The residents gossiped about any crime that did take place for weeks afterward. The town had a grocery, a butcher, a bakery, a hardware store, a tailor, a Sheriff and one part time deputy, and a Doctor. The ocean was an easy bike ride from town. What more could they need?

The larger town of Walton was only a few miles up the road. Walton had department stores, a train station, and a real hospital. Meg loved the harbor in Walton. She loved the ocean even more. Oh, to be on one of those boats going out into that vast expanse! She'd dreamed of it since she was a small child, and her family had come to visit Gran. She contented herself with going to the beach sometimes and observing the ocean from the shore. But one day... one day... she would go out on a boat and see it up close.

Meg and Gran arrived at church to find it decorated for fall. Pumpkins adorned the Remembrance Table and the edges of the platform. Leaves, in clusters, draped over the windows. Potted red and orange mums had been placed in the window sills. Gran led the way to her spot. She'd been sitting in that spot for as long as anyone could remember. Before that, her father sat in that spot. Meg couldn't help chuckling to herself each time they claimed that seat and wondering what might happen if someone else sat there before they did. What on earth would Gran do? She probably wouldn't hear a word of the sermon because she would be thinking so hard about not sitting in the right place.

The service went by in a blur. Meg had trouble concentrating on the sermon. The warm sun and soft breeze blowing in the open windows dragged her attention away again and again. Finally, they stood for the last song. Then the parishioners filed out of the doors into the glorious sunshine. As they left for home, Nellie fell into step beside her. Meg could tell she was bursting with some sort of news, but Nellie was bound to keep it in for some strange and uncharacteristic reason.

"Isn't the weather wonderful?" Nellie asked.

Meg grinned. "I'm enjoying it. We're hoping to get the last of the apples off the trees this week. I can see days and days of work ahead making them up into butter and jam and preserves and canning them for pie filling. Gran says that she doesn't want to bother with it again, but I know she'll change her mind when I suggest giving them away so they don't spoil."

Nellie burst into laughter at this. It happened that way every year. "Maybe I can come over later this week and help. That would be such fun."

"It always makes it go faster," Meg agreed.

Gran and Aunt Elaine walked ahead of them. Gran was talking animatedly about something. Meg figured it was a story about something Aunt Elaine had heard before since she was smiling politely and looking straight ahead. Thankfully, Gran didn't notice. She rarely did these days.

The smell of the roast in the oven met them at the door as they arrived home. Meg's stomach growled, though no one else seemed to notice.

"I'll finish lunch," she said, going straight to the kitchen. She grabbed an apron off the back of the kitchen door as she entered. Nellie was right behind her.

"Seems like I haven't seen you in forever, even though it's only been a week!" said Nellie as she counted plates from the cupboard. "We got a letter from Dad this week."

Uncle Daniel, a doctor, was working in a hospital in Boston, treating those sick of the Spanish Flu.

"I'm sure you are relieved," said Meg. "How is he? Is he still healthy?"

"I think so," Nellie answered. "He didn't have a lot of time to write. He said they work hard. It seems like no matter how much they do, there is always more waiting for them. Every day more and more sick people are brought in, only to die. He said he knows now why they usually only let younger men do those jobs. He sounded weary."

"I'm sure he is. I can't even imagine." Meg frowned at the thought of her uncle working so hard with no end in sight. "Is your Aunt Elaine still writing him every day?"

Nellie smiled a distant, dreamy smile. "Of course! He said he looks forward to getting her letters, though they usually come in bundles, not one at a time. He said that he always has to be careful to figure out the first one to read and go from there, or the news is confusing. Oh, the peas are boiling! Better go set the table!" She was off like a flash, moving the peas from the burner and rushing to the other room to finish putting things on the dining room table.

Meg and Gran always ate in the kitchen, but there wasn't room when more people came to visit. However, the dining room table was too big. The group seemed small when only four sat there. So many people gone. So many missing. Meg shook herself. The day was too beautiful to dwell on sadness and loss. She was going to enjoy it. And she would somehow wheedle the news out of Nellie.

Meg finished putting the roast on the platter and slicing it. She arranged the potatoes and carrots around it. Then, when the girls finished setting out the food, they went to find Gran and Aunt Elaine and get everyone settled at the table.

Chapter Three

"Delicious, as always, Mom," said Aunt Elaine. She wiped her lips on the napkin, careful not to leave any of her lipstick on it. Then she leaned back from the table.

"Like I told you, I heard from Daniel," Aunt Elaine continued, moving from the light conversation they'd been having to something more serious. "He thinks that Nellie needs to get involved in some sort of volunteer work at the hospital."

Gran looked horrified. "He wants her to come to help him? With all the sickness running rampant in Boston?"

Aunt Elaine shook her head. "No, that wouldn't be appropriate or safe. Still, there aren't a lot of ways for a young woman to help. He suggested we check with the hospital in Walton to see if there was anything she could do there. Turns out, they need volunteers there almost every day to take care of small tasks so the hospital staff doesn't have to do them. As you might know," and here she turned to look at Meg and Nellie, "the hospital has more patients than they can handle right now. They need all the help they can get. They are also expecting injured soldiers returning from overseas at any time. Nellie is going to start volunteering sometime in the next week or two. What would you think of Meg helping as well? She could ride with Nellie when she goes. They would only be going two or three days a week for a few hours at a time."

"I don't know." Gran hesitated. "Meg has plans for this week, anyway. We were going to get the rest of the apples picked and put up. After that... Well, I'll have to think about it."

"You think about it all you need, Mom. But let me know as soon as you can so we can make plans." Aunt Elaine smiled at Gran and then at Meg. "I do hope you will join Nellie."

The girls didn't have a chance to talk until they were washing the lunch dishes.

"I'm about to burst with excitement," Nellie gasped when they were alone. "What do you think? Wouldn't it be fun? And *so* romantic, too! Nursing injured soldiers! We'd be like Red Cross nurses or something!" Nellie giggled.

Meg rolled her eyes at her cousin. "Is this the secret you were keeping earlier?" she asked.

"Yes! Mom told me I couldn't say a word to you until she talked with Gran herself. Are you interested?"

"I don't know," Meg said. "It's a new idea for me. I'm not sure I'm all that great around sick people." She thought back to weeks spent in a hospital waiting for her parents to recover. Just the thought of those days could conjure the smells and sounds that had become familiar.

"You'll be fine." Nellie sounded far more enthusiastic about it than Meg felt. "Besides, I'll be there if you get squeamish or anything. My dad is a doctor. I don't think I'd ever have a problem with sick people. Think about it. It could be fun, especially if we're together!"

Meg wasn't sure 'fun' was the word she would use to describe volunteer work. But maybe it was her duty. It would be a way to get out. She rarely left Hollis. Besides, the harbor was in Walton. If she went with them to the hospital, they'd drive by it every time they went. That would almost be worth it.

"Gran's getting worse, isn't she?" asked Nellie.

The statement took Meg by surprise. "I don't understand what you mean."

"She took complete credit for the meal today."

"Gran did fix the meal today," Meg said. "I did little things like shelling the peas and peeling the potatoes – things she has a hard time doing herself. She is a wonderful cook, you know. Don't be too hard on her. She forgets things, but somehow she always manages to do a better job in the kitchen than I do."

The dishes were done, so the two girls went outside to enjoy the afternoon warmth. They had grown up hundreds of miles apart, Nellie living here near Gran and Pop, Meg living in Ohio. They only saw each other when Meg would come for a summer visit now and then. Nellie had been spoiled as a child. When she was a baby, she'd almost died of measles. Uncle Daniel and Aunt Elaine had babied her for many years. She'd gotten over the worst of her irritating habits, but still liked to be the center of attention, have the loudest laughter in the room, the prettiest dresses, the most fabulous hair. Here in their small town, that usually wasn't difficult, but Meg wondered how things would go if they were in Walton.

Later that evening as she prepared for bed, Meg had to admit to herself that dealing with sick people didn't bother her. She didn't want to deal with painful memories. She'd spent time in a hospital once, and the memories from that still gave her nightmares. The thought of going back in and remembering…it was almost too much to contemplate.

Meg knew that Aunt Elaine and Nellie meant well.

At supper this evening Gran brought up the volunteer work all on her own. Meg was surprised she remembered.

"It can't be good for you to be stuck in a house with a little old woman all the time," Gran said, looking off into the distance. Then she looked at Meg. "You need to get out. Live life. Remember what it's like to be a young woman. You stay in town here too much. Going to Walton would be good for you."

"You think I ought to go?" Meg couldn't hide her surprise. "I thought you'd want to keep me around here." Meg knew Gran got lonesome even when Meg wasn't gone long, like a trip the grocery store.

"It will be good for me," Gran insisted. "I've gotten entirely too dependent on you being here. Besides. Mrs. Nelson is next door and she comes every week to quilt with me. The Stuart girl wants to

16

come over and learn to sew. She can come another day. Pretty soon, there will be so many in and out that I won't even notice you're gone."

Meg smiled to herself in the darkness of her room at the memory of Gran's enthusiasm. She was pretty sure it wouldn't be quite like that. Gran would indeed know she was gone. But she knew Gran well enough to know that she was looking at it as a challenge. Meg decided to look at it that way, too. Going into the hospital the first time would be a challenge, but she could overcome it. Soon it wouldn't even be hard anymore. Everything would be normal and familiar. She'd meet new people. Make new friends.

And see the harbor every day.

Yes, that alone was worth the pain of that first time going into the hospital. To see the ocean. She'd give it a try, at least for a little while.

Chapter Four

Meg woke with a start. She stretched. As usual she could smell coffee. It didn't matter how early she woke, Gran was always awake first in the morning. The coffee would be ready. Gran would be putting her feet up enjoying a cup of it in her easy chair in the front room. As part of their morning ritual, Meg would get a cup and join her by the large picture window. They would sit there quietly, sipping their coffee and watching the morning sun light up the sky with its promise of another beautiful fall day.

Meg slipped out of bed and dressed. She braided her thick brown hair and hurried down stairs. They had a big day ahead of them. The rest of the apples wouldn't pick themselves.

Nellie interrupted the quiet morning when she arrived to help with the picking, accompanied by loud laughter and a constant stream of chatter. She breezed into the house, put her bag down and took off her sweater. The chatter continued as the two young women went out to the shed, got the ladder, and set it up by one of the apple trees.

Meg and Gran had cleared the apples from the bottom of the tree the previous week. They couldn't reach the rest without the ladder.

Gran was terrified the girls would hurt themselves on the ladder. She didn't want to watch them work, but she was so worried she sat on the back porch and called out instructions to be careful, watch their step, don't lean out too far or climb up too high. After watching for a long time, she joined them in the yard. Two of the women collected the apples as the third handed them down.

They stopped for a picnic lunch, and finished it with the crunchy, sweet goodness they were picking off the tree. They'd finished one tree and only had the other to do in the afternoon.

"Hullo!" called a man's voice from the front of the house. All three women stopped eating to listen in puzzlement.

"Is someone here?" wondered Meg aloud. She stood up and walked to the gate. A tall, handsome man came around the corner of the house.

Nellie joined her at the gate. Meg watched Nellie look the man over, from the top of his dark-haired head to his shiny dress shoes. She dropped her chin and smiled up at the man through long eyelashes that fluttered ever so slightly.

Meg watched the man grin back at Nellie. Then his gaze shifted back to Meg.

"Please come in," Meg said and gave the man a polite smile. She opened the gate so he could enter. "We've been working in the orchard all morning and are taking a break for lunch. Would you like an apple fresh from the tree?"

"That sounds delicious," the man said. He followed Meg and Nellie across the yard to where Gran sat on her stool. Nellie settled herself on the picnic blanket so the man could see her best side. She smoothed her skirt. Meg sank onto the blanket, stifling a sigh. She asked the man to join them and offered him an apple. He took the apple, seated himself, then faced Gran.

"You must be Mrs. Hollister. I'm Dr. Coburg, Dr. Grey's new assistant." He offered Gran his hand.

"I see," was Gran's curt reply. She looked from the hand to the man's face and back. Finally, she shook it. "These are my granddaughters, Meg and Nellie. I didn't know Dr. Grey needed an assistant. Is he well? Is he still planning to practice here? The town is so small I can't imagine he'd need much help."

Dr. Coburg smiled at the three women. "Dr. Grey is well. I'm working with him for a while to learn how to run a private practice in a small town like this. He said he'd like to get away with his wife and family now and then. A doctor can't do that unless there is someone else to cover for him while he is away."

Dr. Coburg took a bite of his apple and hummed his enjoyment. The bite gave Nellie the opportunity she'd been wanting.

"Where are you from?" she asked, smiling and leaning forward. Before he had a chance to reply she went on. "Hollis is a quiet town. We don't have much going on in the way of entertainment, but I have friends in Walton. If you ever want a break from small town life, I can show you around."

"I grew up not far from here so know my way around, but thanks for the kind offer. My Mom is quite the social butterfly. We were always at some society engagement or another. I'm looking forward to small town life as a break from all that." Dr. Coburg smiled at the three women.

"Where are you staying?" asked Gran.

"In an apartment at the back of the Miller's store. It's not big, but it works well for a bachelor. Dr. Grey has a small amount of space in his office for me to work with him. So far it's working out well, though I have yet to see a patient."

Nellie gave a sharp intake of breath and gripped Meg's arm at the doctor's revelation of bachelorhood. Meg rolled her eyes. Dr. Coburg didn't seem to notice their exchange.

He stayed a few minutes longer, then excused himself. He was barely out of earshot when Nellie burst out talking with excitement.

"Think of it!" she squealed. "A handsome, young, single *doctor* come to live in our town! Oh, Daddy would be so proud of me to marry a doctor – just like him!" She clasped her hands in front of her.

Meg sprang to her feet. "I can't believe you! You are so presumptuous, Nellie! How do you know he doesn't have a girl back home? How do you know he is even interested in getting married right now? How do you know your parents would even approve? For that matter, what gives you the right to decide for him that you are the girl for him to marry? You don't know anything about him!"

Meg whirled away and walked back to the apple trees.

"You're jealous that he noticed me and not you," Nellie mocked her.

Meg stopped. Her hands fisted by her sides. She would *not* grace that with a comment.

"I can't say he really noticed either of you girls," Gran stated. She shoved herself to her feet and gathered the dishes and food to take to the house. "He seemed especially interested in me. He *was* a handsome man, you have to admit that, Meg. Don't worry about the dishes, girls. I'll take care of them." She turned and carried everything into the house.

The girls finished their work in silence that afternoon, a contrast to the joviality of the morning. The rain clouds that rolled in as they were finishing, matched Meg's mood. Nellie left for home as quickly as she could after they were finished, making excuses about beating the rain. She wouldn't look Meg in the eye.

The day had been long. Meg wasn't hungry for supper that night. She listened as Gran talked about her plans for the apples. Meg knew the two of them could get them finished this week. Then she had the hospital volunteer work starting next week. With Nellie. She sighed at the thought.

Meg was too tired to think that night as she fell into bed. Her arms, neck, and back were sore. She had a sunburn.

In those final moments before falling asleep, she realized what was bothering her. She was jealous of Nellie. What Nellie said earlier was true. Nellie had always gotten the boys to pay attention to her.

Meg felt invisible.

Up to now it hadn't mattered, but for some reason this time it did. In the morning it probably wouldn't matter as much as it did now. She was tired. It had been a long day.

Meg rolled onto her side, unable to stop the lone tear from sliding down her cheek as she drifted to sleep because she couldn't stay awake any longer.

Chapter Five

Rain pattered on the roof and windows all night, and Meg slept longer than she intended in the morning. She woke abruptly, sat up, and winced. Her muscles weren't as sore as the day before, but her sunburn hurt worse. A look in the mirror showed that she was probably going to peel on her nose and cheeks, the back of her neck, and maybe even on her forearms. Why hadn't she thought to wear a hat? Nellie had worn one and so had Gran. Now she would have a tan. Nellie's skin was always creamy and white. Her hair was always in place. With her fair coloring and pink cheeks, no wonder men noticed her. Meg, on the other hand, hadn't ever cared that much.

She dressed and stared at herself in the mirror while she brushed her hair and pinned it up. With another long day of work ahead of her, Meg didn't want to have to worry about her hair getting in the way.

The morning was cold and dreary, but Gran and Meg warmed the house as they cooked. The delicious smell of the apples cooking permeated every room. Meg felt as if she were in heaven.

By Friday, they both had a different opinion about apples. When they'd poured last of it in a hot jar and the lid and ring were secured on top waiting to seal, Meg fell into a chair. "If I ever see another apple in my whole life, it will be too soon," she said with a relieved sigh.

Gran chuckled. "You said that the last two years and still did it again this year. I don't blame you. We had a good crop of apples this year. Now, we ought to take some of these preserves over to Elaine and Nellie."

Meg sighed again. She wasn't ready to see Nellie. Not yet.

Gran gently patted Meg on the arm. "Monday is coming up pretty quick. You girls have to work together. We'd better get things patched up between you. Here, wrap this warm loaf of bread, and we'll walk over there. The fresh air will do us both some good. By the time we get back the last jars should be sealed."

Meg enjoyed the walk in the crisp fall air. The rain earlier in the week had cooled the temperature without spoiling the trees. Meg relished the explosion of color around them.

Aunt Elaine was happy for the preserves. Nellie was no where in sight. Meg sank onto the couch with relief.

They had been visiting for a while when Nellie breezed into the house, all smiles. She acted as though nothing had happened on Monday. Meg chided herself for wasting so much time being irritated.

At the first opportunity, Nellie dragged Meg into her room. She shut the door, giggling with excitement.

"I saw him again! Well, admittedly I made up an excuse to go to the grocery this morning, so I could see him before he left." Nellie was all smiles. "He remembered my name and said he'd probably see us at the hospital on Monday! He is *so* handsome! Such a gentleman! He walked with me as far as Dr. Grey's office and even took my arm when we crossed the street."

"That's wonderful." Meg pasted on a smile and tried to act happy. Now she remembered why she'd been irritated.

"What should I wear on Monday? What are you going to wear? I want to look nice, but not over dressed for helping in a hospital. Is the green dress the right thing, do you think? It would make my eyes stand out, but doesn't look too fussy." Nellie prattled on and on. She took one dress after the other out of her closet to see if they were what she was looking for.

Meg had never dreamed of having that many clothes. She stifled a groan and grimaced at Nellie's back in annoyance.

"What about this dress?" Nellie spun around, holding a dress up to herself.

"I'm sure it will be fine. You look good in anything you wear." Meg plastered the smile in place in the nick of time.

"I know, I know," Nellie agreed. "But I need to look just right. Here, let's go through these one by one."

Meg felt the next hour would never end. She knew nothing she said would convince Nellie one way or other and, quite honestly, she didn't care.

"Meg!" Aunt Elaine's voice called up the hallway. "Gran needs to go home. Are you two about done in there?"

Meg bounded to her feet and across the room to the door.

Nellie sighed. "I didn't make a decision. I mean, this dress would work, but the shoes are too fussy and that dress is too much, but maybe if I wore this necklace it would look better..."

"I really must go," Meg interrupted, hand on the doorknob, relieved to have an excuse to leave. "Gran has been working hard for the past several days. I'm sure her arthritis is bothering her. I know whatever you decide will be perfect." She plastered the smile on again and opened the door. "See you Sunday!" Then she hurried down the hall as fast as she could before Nellie could call her back.

Chapter Six

Monday morning dawned gray. Heavy clouds threatened rain. The weather suited Meg's mood. She questioned her decision to volunteer as soon as she woke that morning. She felt grumpy, nervous, and wished she could call the whole thing off.

With a panicked sensation in the pit of her stomach, she looked in her wardrobe to see what she would wear. She hadn't picked the night before in her own little protest against the over planning ways of her cousin. Now she wished she had not protested so much.

Coffee might help. Meg stumped downstairs in her housecoat and slippers.

"Not dressed yet?" Gran asked in surprise as Meg stumped into the front room with her coffee cup in hand. "Are you feeling well?"

"I'm fine. Just nervous. And scared. Oh, Gran! Why did I ever agree to do this?" Meg moaned as she sank into her chair by the window and drew her knees up to her chest. "I haven't been back to a hospital since, well, you know." She moaned again.

"Ah, dear. You'll be fine. What is the biggest problem at this moment?"

Meg loved it when Gran asked that. It made all problems, no matter how big, drift into the background as she focused on the one bothering her most.

"I don't know what to wear," Meg said. "I can't figure out what kind of clothes would be appropriate. If I was visiting someone, I'd dress up. If I was cleaning, I'd dress in my worst clothes. But I don't know what I'm going to be doing. What if I get there, and have to sit and read to some little child in my cleaning dress?" Her face flushed at the embarrassment brought on by the thought alone.

"The way I see it, you should dress for every day. I doubt they'd put you to any hard cleaning on the first day. So you won't need your oldest dress. Wear an every day one, but put your hair up nice. There. Now what's next?" Gran settled back into her chair like she could fix all the world's problems from that little seat.

Meg grinned and relaxed. Gran's suggestion was logical. "I'll be back down in a little bit," she said as she bounced out of her chair, kissed Gran on the cheek and bounded up the stairs to her room. She was ready long before Aunt Elaine drove up to the house.

As she climbed into the back seat, Nellie turned around with her nose all wrinkled up. "You decided to wear that?" she asked in horror and distaste. Nellie was wearing her second best dress and hat, and her best shoes.

Aunt Elaine cut Nellie a look of annoyance as she pulled away from Gran's house. "You don't know what you'll be doing there today."

"I'm sure I'll be taking care of sick soldiers. Or maybe sick children. Maybe we'll even get to help with the babies!"

"In truth, girls, I don't know what you'll be doing, but I doubt it will be caring for patients. The hospital staff takes their responsibilities seriously. I've already told Nellie this, but it bears repeating. Be prepared to do the menial. You might be taking food to rooms and removing it. You might also be mopping halls. They'll give you things to help make the staff's job easier so they can focus on their patients. Nellie, you are far too overdressed for what you'll be doing today."

Nellie tossed her head. "I'm helping them. I'm sure they wouldn't give me anything too unpleasant to do. Besides, a lady must always look her best. You taught me that, Mom."

"You need to be prepared for anything," her mother chided her. "And you aren't. They won't believe you are willing to work if you come dressed like that every day. I don't know who you are trying to impress, but it won't work like you think it will."

26

Meg looked out the car window. She didn't get to ride in a car often. Uncle Daniel had one so he could call on patients who lived away from Hollis. Aunt Elaine had learned to drive it before he'd left. Even then, she didn't drive often. Meg always thought it would be wonderful to drive, especially one of those cars with no top. Well, not on a rainy day like today. But on a lovely summer day, breezing along with the wind in your hair. Yes, that would be nice.

At almost any turn now she'd be able to see the ocean. She looked between the trees to catch the first glimpse. In spite of the gray skies and the rain, the ocean made her catch her breath. Fog hovered in the distance. She could see ships tossing on the choppy waves. The white capped waves crashed into the rocky shore. The thought of being in one of those boats in weather like this made her nervous, but just once she wanted to try it. The tangy smell of the salt air reached her nose. She could almost taste the saltiness of the ocean. The crashing waves were mesmerizing. Before she knew it they were coming near the harbor and into town.

The nervous, sick, sinking feeling flooded back into the pit of her stomach. They pulled up next to the curb in front of the hospital. This was it. There was no going back now. Meg squared her shoulders as she walked up the steps to the door. She'd never been a quitter.

Meg stepped into the hospital lobby. The sounds, smells, and sights that greeted her were almost overwhelming. Her eyes slid shut as the sound of wheelchairs on the tile floor, the smell of the cleaning soap, the cry of a baby in the distance, a man coughing, all brought back memories that she had tried to tuck away.

In her mind's eye, she could see another hospital, hundreds of miles away, and two very sick people lying in a room together. She could see the grave looks on the doctor's faces, the nurses bustling about trying to comfort a terrified young woman, who was also sick. She could smell the odors of illness, mixed with medicine and soap. She felt the hopelessness that had come when the fight was lost by one of those people, only to have another dear person fall ill and fill that bed, then lose their fight as well. A tear squeezed out of her eye and slid down her cheek. Remembering was almost as painful as the actual events.

A gentle squeeze on her arm brought Meg back to the present. She opened her eyes and met Aunt Elaine's smiling sympathetic ones staring back, at her. Meg shook herself and tried to clear her mind.

The hospital manager, a cheerful lady in a dark dress, arrived a moment later to greet them.

"Hello. My name is Miss Nichols. If you will, please follow me." Miss Nichols took them into a side waiting room. "How can I help you?"

"I'm Elaine Greene. My husband, Dr. Greene, was supposed to have contacted you about my daughter and niece volunteering here." Aunt Elaine indicated the two young women waiting and then turned back to Miss Nichols with a smile.

"Ah! Yes, he did contact us about it. Let me find the matron so these ladies can get their assignment. We need all the help we can get right now. Please, wait here. I'll be back in a moment." Miss Nichols left.

She returned a few minutes later with a nurse. Miss Nichols introduced them to Nurse Rogers. "I'll leave you to her capable care. She will be giving you assignments and supervising your work."

Nurse Rogers stepped into the hallway. "Please follow me." Without waiting for an answer, she turned and walked out of the waiting room and into the hospital wards. She looked like she was middle aged. Her dark, gray-streaked hair was pulled severely back into a bun. Her white dress was starched until it would stand on its own. The careful and proper steps of her prim white shoes clicked across the tile floor. There would be no funny business of any kind on her watch. Meg would have been afraid of her – if there hadn't been that little twinkle behind her hazel eyes and the smile wrinkles around her mouth.

Nurse Rogers was talking, pointing out the various wards, for children, for the very sick, for pregnant women or women who'd delivered babies, for injured people. She pointed to the laundry, the kitchen, the nurses' office, a doctor's office.

28

"Most of the patients started coming in two weeks ago. It's that infernal flu that has killed so many already. Since then, we have more people than this hospital was designed to handle. The patient rooms have as many beds in them as they will hold, more than is comfortable. We expect more soldiers back from Europe at any time. We can barely keep up with laundry or medicine. The staff is stretched thin. We appreciate any help we can get, but you have to be willing to roll up your sleeves and do anything that needs doing." Nurse Rogers stopped walking and talking. She looked Nellie up and down. "There will be many jobs for you to do as often as you can come, but I'm starting you with something that has become the most urgent." She turned to Aunt Elaine. "Are you staying to help as well today?" she asked.

Aunt Elaine looked sad and shook her head. "No. I'm sorry, but I can't. Not today. I will as many days as I'm able."

"In that case, I'll say goodbye and get these two young women busy. The sooner they get to work the better."

Nurse Rogers turned without another word and led the way up the hallway nearest to them. Nellie and Meg waved quickly to Aunt Elaine, then rushed to follow her.

Nurse Rogers brought them to a small room with stark white walls and two open windows high up in the wall. If the windows hadn't been open the room would have been stuffy. As it was, it was cool and damp. A sewing machine and thread sat on a table near the wall. On a wooden table in the corner, Columns of sheets were stacked almost to the ceiling on a wooden table in the corner. Two nurses worked frantically, ripping the sheets from one of the stacks into strips and sewing the strips together for bandaging. They both looked up as the women entered.

Nurse Rogers addressed the two nurses. "These women are here to volunteer in the hospital today. They can take care of these sheets so you can get back to the ward."

Relief washed over their faces as they stopped what they were doing and moved toward the door. "You will need to show them what to do, however." Both nurses stopped and looked at the women standing in front of them.

It only took a few minutes for Meg and Nellie to get the instructions. Tear the sheets into strips. Sew the strips together end to end. How hard could that be? Nurse Rogers waited until the nurses left before she continued talking. Another large stack of sheets needed to be mended. They had enough work to keep them busy for a long time.

"You can eat lunch in the dining room here in the hospital, or there are diners just up the street. The sheets need to be fixed by this evening. There will be more tomorrow. We are expecting so many patients - soldiers from the front with terrible wounds, many of them burns and infections. We need as many bandages as we can get as fast as you can get them done. We're not sure when the soldiers will be arriving so work as fast as possible. Again, thank you so much for your help." For the first time her lips twitched up into a smile as she left, closing the door behind her.

The girls stood for a moment and stared at the huge stack, then at the sewing machine, and then at each other. They removed their coats and hats, and hung them on hooks behind the door. Meg moved toward the table and picked up the sheet the nurse had abandoned. Nellie took her cue, and moved to the sewing machine. She began working the treadle, sewing the strips that Meg tore, and mending sheets in between.

"Mom was right. I'm sorely overdressed," she sighed. She made no effort to keep the irony out of her voice. "I should have known better. He'll never find us here in this closet of a room at the back of the hospital."

Meg felt a twinge of sympathy for her cousin. She smiled. "We didn't come today to try to catch a man," she reminded Nellie.

"Speak for yourself!" Nellie chuckled and reached for another strip.

Time seemed to stand still that morning. It didn't seem to matter how many strips were torn or how many sheets were mended, there was always another item in the stack. After an hour or two Meg's arms ached from the motion of tearing over and over again.

Nellie sat up straighter and stretched her back with a small moan. They looked at each other and, without a word, switched places. Sewing wasn't much better, but at least it gave her arms a break. After some time had passed they stopped to wrap the bandages into rolls, trimming the strings on the edges.

"Mom and Gran would die of mortification if they saw these so disheveled," Nellie muttered as she concentrated on removing the worst of the strings from the roll. "We should hem them, but we don't have time." They still needed to fold the pile of mended sheets and stack them neatly in another place.

They switched again. Meg looked at the stack, knowing that somehow those sheets were reproducing themselves. It looked no smaller than it had when they'd begun.

Nurse Rogers came for the bandages and sheets at midday and seemed pleased with the progress. She exclaimed over the tidy rolls and was overjoyed that there were so many of them. "You best take a break for lunch," she commented as she left the room, closing them in again.

Meg had not even considered that they would need lunch. She looked at Nellie. Nellie had already picked up her purse and was digging through the contents. "I know I have some money in here left over from what Mom gave me for the grocery the other day. I'm starving! I can't wait until supper tonight to eat something. I'm sure there is enough for both of us. She won't mind if we use it." She produced the money with a flourish. Both girls reached for their hats and coats.

They walked to a cafe up the road from the hospital in a steady drizzle of rain. By the time they reached it, they were chilled through. Nellie had just enough money to buy soup and a sandwich each. They ate in silence. Suddenly Nellie chuckled. "We get all this time to spend together and we don't say a word all day."

"I know." Meg shook her head and looked into her soup. "I was shocked when I saw that huge pile of sheets. I know that no matter how long we work today, we'll hardly make a dent."

Nellie nodded agreement. "I came today expecting to be doing all these noble things. Like caring for little children and stroking comfort onto some fevered brow." She sighed. "I suppose having clean bandages is noble for those who really need them. It's just so... so..."

"Overwhelming." Meg finished for her. "But I'm way too stubborn to quit. I'd love to get to the bottom of at least one of those stacks before we leave today."

"Yeah, like that's going to happen." Nellie rolled her eyes.

"It could. Maybe. We have to keep going at it like we have been." Meg sounded far more confident than she felt.

They finished and trudged back through the rain to the little workroom in the hallway. They gave each other a look that held both trepidation and challenge, then started back into the work as hard as they could. As the afternoon wore on, the bottom of the first stack came closer and closer. They worked faster and more efficiently. Nurse Rogers came in now and then to get the finished rolls of bandages or clean, mended sheets. Aside from her, they saw no one.

When Aunt Elaine arrived late in the afternoon both girls were exhausted, but satisfied. All but one of the sheets on that first stack were torn into bandages and they'd mended all the sheets. They were rather pleased with themselves.

"So, how was it?" asked Aunt Elaine the two silent young women in her automobile. They looked at each other.

Nellie chuckled. "I was definitely overdressed. And I lost the shoes halfway through the day so I'd still be able to walk when you got there."

Meg chuckled, too. "And we found out that we won't be seeing people."

"But it's okay," Nellie continued for them. "It felt like we accomplished something today, even though we barely made a dent."

"It could be because it is so meaningful for the people who need it," Meg added. "We will need to be sure to bring lunch every day. That shouldn't be hard. Gran is always eager to over feed me when I'm going to be away for lunch." She grinned at the thought.

"Who knows, maybe we'll even meet some people instead of seeing four walls, two windows and a door all day," said Nellie.

"And a table, stack of sheets, and a sewing machine," Meg added. "Then you'll wish you'd have worn those shoes again." she chucked.

"Not on your life!" stated Nellie emphatically. "Mom will be lucky to get me to wear these to church again!"

Gran was eager to hear all about her day and Meg was eager to tell it. They lingered at the kitchen table as they talked about their day apart. She told about the pile of sheets, the sewing machine in the little room, and the host of new patients that the hospital could barely contain. She told about how they made it almost through that huge stack by sheer grit and determination.

Gran had been busy today, too. The Stuart's oldest daughter had come over to learn to sew. The fruit of their hard, frustrating labor was sitting by the sewing machine in the next room in the form of an apron that didn't have a straight seam in it. According to Gran, she had two left hands and was quite dense. Meg laughed out loud at Gran's description of them working together.

"How was it going back into a hospital after all this time?" Gran asked as they cleaned the supper dishes together.

"It was hard. Very hard. I almost turned and left," Meg confessed. "But I have to face it sometime. It made the pain so fresh and real again. It's only been two years."

"I know, dearie." Gran gently patted her arm after she finished wiping her hands on a towel. "It might not get easier for a while. But you'll learn to get around it. Then it won't be the first thing you think of every time."

Meg hoped with all her heart that was true.

Chapter Seven

The screaming woke Jack out of a fitful sleep yet again. A nun in a white and blue habit stood over him. Her wimple accentuated her crows feet and the smile lines around her mouth. She was not, however, smiling at Jack.

"Hush," she said in a heavily accented whisper. "You must not wake the others."

Jack had never known such pain. Waves of white hot agony washed over him. He clenched his fists and gritted his teeth against the cry that threatened to force its way out, despite his best efforts otherwise.

"You must be steadfast," the nun whispered. She wiped Jack's face with a cool damp cloth and fluffed his pillow. "You are one of the blessed."

Jack managed a snort and stifled the groan that followed. "Hard to see how I'm blessed." Another wave of pain. Jack twisted on the bed, bared his teeth, clenched his eyes shut. "I can't live like this. I wish I'd just have died."

The nun wiped his face again. She swiped away the tears that trickled down Jack's face and into his hair.

"You have eyes that can still see. Some men have lost their eyes from the gas or from enemy fire. You have both hands and both feet. Some men have none. You have good lungs, untouched by the gas. Others do not. If they live to see their home and family, they will struggle every day to breathe and work. No, you should be happy to be alive." She wiped his face again.

"Why didn't they cut my legs off? I can't deal with this pain."

"The matron will come soon and give you medicine for the pain."

"Can't you put that cool cloth on my legs? I'm begging."

"The nurse will wash them. Soon. Very soon."

Jack cried out as the fiery agony washed over him again. The nun gripped his shoulder and pressed him back onto the bed.

"Cut. Them. Off," Jack hissed through clenched teeth.

"Why? You will heal. You will walk again."

"I can't. I can't. It's unbearable. It hurts too bad."

Though he was embarrassed to do so, Jack couldn't stop the sobs that wracked his body. He turned away from the gentle nun and buried his face in the blanket roll he used for a pillow. When he turned back to look, the nun was gone, leaving Jack to his dark thoughts.

$$\infty$$

As weeks passed, Jack discovered he'd been brought to a convent near the sea. He also discovered he was, indeed, one of the blessed. Miraculously, the gas had burned only his legs. Weeks of disuse caused the muscle to shrivel and atrophy. The doctor insisted bandages would only bring on gangrene. Instead, his legs were left open to the air. Large blisters covered them. They burst and seeped yellow liquid until the sheet was wet with it. Then they dried and his legs would stick, painfully, to the sheets. The convent had limited medicine. They could only give him something for the pain at night and sometimes, if the Red Cross supplies were late, they saved the medicine for the men with the worst injuries.

When Jack could manage, he tried to sit up and look around him. It distracted him from the continual burning in his legs. He noticed others who were far worse off than he was. One man was covered in gas burns over every part of his body that Jack could see. He didn't move except to moan and clutch at the bed, a gesture Jack found surprisingly soothing.

One side of another man's body had been blown apart from shrapnel. His arm and leg were gone, as was part of his face. Deep red gouges covered his side where the doctors had sewn him shut. Jack couldn't understand how this man had lived through his ordeal or how he would go on and live his life afterward.

Another man's head had been partially caved in when the trench collapsed on him. The nun said he wasn't blind. Nonetheless, he stared into space as though he was. He could chew and swallow the food a nun put to his mouth. Sometimes, he'd turn his vacant stare in the direction of whomever was caring for him. He'd blink. Then his eyes would return to the place on the ceiling that interested him most.

"How are they going to manage at home?" Jack asked the nun who brought him his lunch most days. She didn't know much English and gave a shake of her head and a pat on his shoulder, handed him his bowl of thin soup, and moved on to the next man.

The only time the burned man cried out was when they washed his wounds. Jack would watch in perverse fascination. He didn't know how the burned man could lie so still, how he only allowed soft cries to escape as they washed him. When they finished, the man would heave deep breaths and lie back in relief. He'd nod and murmur to the orderlies attending him.

Jack's own agony awaited him when his turn came. He had to fight back screams. He wanted to punch every one of the orderlies helping him. Instead, he retreated deep within himself. He thought of his parent's farm in Indiana. He wondered what they knew of his condition. He wondered what they would say when they saw him again, when they found out he'd never walk again. How could he walk on these shriveled, blistered, sorry excuses for legs and feet?

They finished. Oh, the blessed relief of it. The pain would diminish back to its normal white, hot agony levels. Sometimes they'd even give him medicine to reduce the pain. Jack didn't know if the medicine really took care of the pain, or if it just made him able to ignore it. He didn't care. He longed for the medicine all day, every day. If there wasn't enough, if supplies were low, he allowed himself to sob quietly into his bed roll once the room was dark for the night. He knew it wasn't manly but he didn't care.

$$\infty$$

"You will be able to travel to London, then to America on the next troop transport," the doctor stated without looking up from Jack's chart.

Jack looked up at him, surprised.

"What, you thought we'd heal you and send you back to the front?" the doctor continued with a chuckle. "You'll be happy to hear your fighting days are over. From what I've gathered, they are hoping everyone will be finished fighting before long."

Jack shook his head. "I never thought I'd go back. I can't walk."

"Give it time. You should make a near full recovery. You'll always have to be careful of the scar tissue."

Jack winced. "I can't walk. It hurts too much."

"Yes, it still does, I'm sure. It will for a while yet. But I'd be surprised if you never walked again. Your bones weren't damaged by the mustard gas, just your soft tissue. You should be able to build back the muscle you've lost." He thumped Jack on the shoulder. "You can't give up. You're one of the lucky ones."

Jack glowered at the doctor.

The doctor regarded Jack for a long moment, then sighed. "You get to leave on the transport. If not tomorrow, then the next day. Good luck."

Chapter Eight

"Beautiful day for sitting out on the deck, wouldn't you say? Fancy us ending up on the same transport."

Jack swung his wheel chair around to face the speaker.

"Lieutenant!" he said, a smile breaking across his face for the first time in weeks. It faded as quickly as it came.

A bandage covered the lieutenant's eyes and both legs were gone below the knee. Jack thought about how many times he'd longed for that same situation. At this exact minute it didn't seem as appealing.

The lieutenant beamed back at him. "I think we're both about to get our discharge papers. You can call me George."

"Is that your name?" Jack asked.

"Nah, but you can call me that."

Jack chuckled before he could stop himself. It felt good. The lieutenant joined him.

"My name really is George," the lieutenant said. "George Stafford. Never thought I'd make lieutenant. They only gave it to me because I was the last person in my unit to make it this long. Well, as long as I made it anyway."

"What happened to you after I left? Got wounded?"

"I caught shrapnel from artillery fire. You know they kept that going day and night. Luck just ran out one day, though I don't believe in luck. Guess it was my time. They had to take off both legs 'cause there wasn't enough left of them to save."

"How'd you find me up here? You can't…" Jack waved his hand in the general direction of his face, then realized his friend couldn't see him.

"I can see through the bandage." George never cracked a smile.

"Seriously?"

George guffawed and slapped his stump. A dot of red bloomed on the bandage and spread rapidly. George didn't notice. An orderly hurried over and wrapped another bandage over the first to stanch the blood flow.

George heaved a contented sigh, then continued. "Nah, one of the orderlies said a guy named Jack Collins always wanted to sit on the deck. I thought 'could it be my own Sergeant Collins?' and decided to check. And here we are. How are you Jack? How are your legs?"

Jack couldn't believe the lieutenant remembered his injury after all this time. "Did you ask the orderly about that, too?"

"Nope, that was all me." George's perpetual grin focused in Jack's direction.

"Not great, I guess. They keep telling me I should be happy to be alive. I'm one of the lucky ones."

"You are. But you don't believe them?"

"How am I lucky with burns like this?"

George waved at his own stumps. "You might be able to walk again."

"I doubt it," Jack muttered. "I'm in pain all the time. It isn't as bad as it was a few weeks ago. It's a constant dull ache, until they clean them. That hurts like nothing I've ever experienced. I come up here to think. The sea reminds me there are things bigger than me and my problems." He sighed and leaned back against the wheel chair. "Besides, it's peaceful. I got used to the waves lapping on the beach at the convent and now I'm having even more trouble than normal sleeping because I miss that sound."

"It is peaceful, isn't it." George turned his face in the direction of the sea. "Have you ever been in the ocean?"

"Nah, we lived too far inland and Dad could never leave the farm. First time I ever saw it was when I shipped out for Europe."

"My folks took us to the beach once when I was a kid. It's one of my favorite memories. There is nothing like the feel of the sand between your toes or the cold waves hitting you for the first time." George took a deep breath through his nose. "And the smell of it. There are few things I can think of that I like better. It stays with you for the rest of your life."

Jack looked at his friend, the stumps sticking out from the edge of the chair, the blood stain that had spread to the new bandages. He had to blink hard to stop the tears from falling.

"I hear we're going to Boston on our way back," Jack finally managed around the lump in his throat. He cleared it and coughed. George didn't seem to notice.

"They had to scrap that plan. Boston has the fever pretty bad. We're going to Portland instead. Have you had the fever?"

Jack nodded, then remembered George couldn't see him. "Got it almost as soon as I arrived here in March. We lost half our unit to the fever, before we even saw any fighting. That's when they combined us with yours."

"I never got it," said George. He shrugged. "I guess that's the least of my worries now. I'm glad we aren't going to Boston."

The blood had soaked through the second bandage, too. An orderly hurried up to them with a doctor.

"We need to get this looked at," said the doctor. "You'll have to excuse us."

"Good to see you, sergeant," said George with a grin.

Jack smiled. "I'm glad we ran into each other like this."

George barked a laugh. "He does have a sense of humor!"

Jack waved at his friend as the orderly wheeled him away, knowing full well George couldn't see him. He gazed back across the sea and wondered what it felt like to put your feet in it. He'd have to find out sometime.

$$\infty$$

The following morning dawned gray, foggy, and cold. Jack endured having his legs washed better than normal. He planned to go in search of George as soon as he'd eaten breakfast.

He choked down the mush they called porridge. Then he wheeled himself around the corridors below decks. He'd made one pass and had started his second when he saw the orderly who had taken George away the previous afternoon. He hurried to where the man was working with another patient.

"I'm looking for George Stafford. Have you seen him this morning?"

The man stopped what he was doing and gave Jack a long look. Something inside Jack recoiled from that look. He drew away.

"What happened?" Jack's voice came out as a whisper.

"They couldn't stop the bleeding. He was still weak from blood loss when he got the injury. His body couldn't take it. He died early this morning."

"No." Jack wheeled his chair further away. "No, he was going to go home and recover. We were going to Portland together."

"I'm sorry man, I really am." The orderly turned back to his patient.

Jack wheeled himself back to his bed and got someone to help him into it. He drew his blanket over himself to block out the cold, the fog, the pain. What point was there in going on when a guy like Lieutenant Stafford died on the ship home?

Chapter Nine

The girls fell into a routine with their volunteer work the next few weeks. Some days they worked steadily at making bandages and mending sheets. Slowly the pile diminished. When it was almost gone, the nurses would bring a fresh supply of sheets from the laundry. Some were too worn to be used again so those were made into bandages. Others needed mending. Aunt Elaine and Gran both managed to find even more sheets to keep the girls busy.

Before they finished that project, Nurse Rogers showed them some other mending that had been piling up. Hospital gowns needed buttons, strings sewed back on, seams repaired. Pants needed the crotches sewed shut again. Pillow cases had worn seams. There were even some white doctor's coats that needed to be fixed.

Other days, they helped in the kitchen. The first day Meg peeled potatoes from a pile almost as tall as she was. At the end of the day, her hands were brown, no matter how much she scrubbed them and she'd rubbed a blister with the knife.

"I think I'm going to give up eating potatoes," she groaned to Gran that evening.

They washed dishes, prepared tea and coffee, chopped vegetables for soup, and swept and mopped the floor over and over. The days they spent sewing seemed easy in comparison to their days in the kitchen.

"Don't they have other volunteers?" Meg asked.

"I've seen others in the dining room, but I've never met them," Nellie said. "It is odd that, with all these new patients, there isn't more help."

"Maybe it's because so many people are or have been sick. Folks might be afraid to come to the hospital because they don't want to get sick, too."

They began eating lunch in the hospital dining room. Most people eating there were those under the hospital's care. Others were staff.

At first, the two young women sat at their own table and chatted. They'd talk about the people in the dining room with them and surmise what was wrong with each one of those convalescing. Sometimes it was obvious. If it wasn't, they constructed elaborate and romantic notions of what could be wrong. Then they'd have to stifle giggles or risk the matron glaring at them from across the room.

One afternoon, two nurses wound their way across the dining room to their table.

"Are these seats taken?"asked the shorter of the two. She had light brown, curly hair that had come loose from her bun under her white cap and hung in wisps around her face. "My name is Phoebe, by the way."

Meg smiled in welcome. "Of course they aren't taken. Please! Sit with us! My name is Meg. This is my cousin, Nellie."

The other girl was tall with dark hair and dark eyes that sparkled in fun. "My name is Sarah," she said as she sat down in the remaining empty chair. "You two must be the wonder women putting out all those bandages and fixing all our linens. We thank you! From the bottom of our heart!"

"Yes! Oh, yes!" Phoebe exclaimed in agreement. "We've been so busy that things had gotten pretty bad. I'm so glad someone is helping us keep up."

"Are all the men in here soldiers back from the front?" asked Nellie looking around the room.

"Most of them," answered Sarah. "They get them patched up enough to make the trip, and then try to keep them alive on the ships to get them back here so we can finish the job. It's so sad. Most of them won't talk about what they've been through or the things they've seen."

"The hardest ones are the ones who breathed in the gas. Their lungs and throats were burned. Most of those didn't live. But if they did live, they have almost constant pain. Some of them can't talk any more. They'll probably be in pain and deal with lung conditions the rest of their lives." Phoebe shook her head as she spoke. "The rest are recovering from influenza. Those are the lucky ones."

Meg's throat tightened and her eyes blurred with tears as she looked at these suffering men. Going to war was bad enough. To watch their friends die, and then spend the rest of their life suffering, well, that was almost unbearable. Nellie's next question brought her back to the conversation. She cleared her throat and took a sip of her water.

"Aren't there other volunteers?" Nellie asked.

"Oh, yes, of course there are. But most of them are older women who have a hard time doing what you are doing," answered Phoebe.

"Or they're too rich to be stuck in a room with a lot of mending or making bandages or cooking." Sarah rolled her eyes as she spoke. "People like helping out when everyone will see it. They can congratulate themselves on their good work, then forget all about it until they need to brag to their friends."

Nellie looked at Meg and her cheeks flushed pink. Meg quickly looked away and hid her smile in the bite of cold ham sandwich she was eating.

"You know I got over my bad attitude about being hid back in a closet," Nellie muttered when they got back to work after lunch.

Meg had to scramble for context, but then it dawned on her what Nellie was talking about. She smiled. "I know. You've done great! Who knows? Maybe after we finish with all this we'll actually get to see people."

Not long after lunch, Nurse Rogers knocked on the open door and poked her head around it. "You girls will need to finish what you are doing right away. Nellie, your mom has arrived to take you home."

The two girls gave each other a look. Meg finished what she was doing, then put her work away for the weekend.

"I hope everything is okay," Meg whispered to Nellie as they hurried to the hospital exit.

"Gran isn't feeling well," explained Aunt Elaine as she drove them home. "I've been with her most of the morning, but she insisted that you come home a little early and help her get to bed. She said she couldn't tolerate staying up any longer."

Meg's forehead furrowed in concern. "How is she unwell?"

"She has developed a cough this afternoon. She said she didn't feel very well when you left, but she wanted you to come to work today. I'm sure she'll be right as rain in the morning." Aunt Elaine smiled her reassurance to Meg.

Chapter Ten

Gran wasn't well in the morning. She was worse. She'd developed a fever over night and didn't feel like getting out of bed. Meg made chicken soup and gave Gran a cup of the stock. She bathed Gran's face and arms in cool water to bring the fever down, with no success.

Sunday came and went with no improvement. Meg only left Gran's side to find food and change the water in the bowl when it got too warm.

Monday morning Meg woke with a jerk. She'd fallen asleep in the chair next to Gran's bed after caring for her most of the night. Gran was struggling to get out of bed and talking nonsense, her body burning up with fever. Meg decided go for Dr. Grey.

Meg tucked Gran back in bed and gave her a drink of water before she left. She knew there was no guarantee Gran would still be there when Meg got home, so she ran as fast as she could through the early morning fog.

She went to the doctor's office first, in a vain hope that Dr. Grey would be in. He wasn't. Of course not. It was too early in the morning. Meg shook her head to clear the sleep deprived fog from her mind. She needed to think clearly and make decisions. Where else should she go?

She ran to Dr. Grey's house, only a block or two away from his Main Street office. The house was silent and dark. Meg pounded on the front door. No one answered. She ran to the back of the house and pounded on the kitchen door. Still no answer. Panicked, she ran again to the front and pounded and yelled, thinking they might still be sleeping. All remained quiet in the house. The next door neighbor came onto his front porch to see what all the commotion was.

"They're gone. Went on a trip to see their daughter in the west. If you need a Doc you'll have to get the other one in town. Dr. Coburg's his name." The middle aged man went back into his house shaking his head and muttering about people making too much noise this early in the morning.

Meg sank onto the front step, trying to stifle panicked sobs. She put her face in her hands. She was so tired and she didn't know how to find Dr. Coburg. Surely he'd found a more permanent place to live than the apartment behind the grocery.

Meg gritted her teeth, squared her shoulders, and set off for the grocery. She hurried to the front of the store and beat on the door. It wouldn't be open for business for several more hours, but she hoped that someone would hear her if she made enough noise. Only a few moments passed before Mr. Miller came to the door and opened the lock.

"Can I help you, Miss Hollister?" he asked of the wild-eyed young woman standing at the door. "We're not open yet, you know."

"I know," Meg answered. "Is Dr. Coburg still living here?"

"Yes, of course! Let me get him for you. Is your Gran alright? I noticed you two didn't go to church yesterday."

His kind tone brought tears to Meg's eyes. Weak from relief that Dr. Coburg was in, Meg sagged against the door. "No, she isn't well. She's been sick since Friday and is only getting worse. I've already left her for too long. Dr. Grey is gone on a trip. I'm sorry to disturb Dr. Coburg at this hour."

Mr. Miller left for a moment and was back with the Doctor. "I heard what you told Mr. Miller. Let's be on our way," he said sensing her urgency.

It seemed like it took an eternity to get back to their street and another eternity to get to the house. Meg did all she could not to run. Her speed surprised the doctor as they hastened through the deserted

48

village streets. She did run up the steps to the house and threw open the front door.

"Come in! Come in!" She called over her shoulder as she disappeared into the back bedroom. Dr. Coburg followed the sound of her voice down the hallway beside the stairs and found a nice sized bedroom. Gran was still in bed, but she wasn't sleeping. When Meg came in, she decided that she must get up. Meg put her hands on Gran's shoulders to keep her in bed, but Gran fought her.

Dr. Coburg took charge. "Mrs. Hollister, you must stay in bed. Your granddaughter tells me that you haven't been feeling well. Let me check you and see how I can help."

"You're that new doctor," Gran said, looking him over through half-shut eyes. "Where is Dr. Grey? He is the only doctor I want to see right now. I won't see anyone but Dr. Grey." The fever caused her to behave like a petulant child.

Dr. Coburg didn't seem phased by her complaints. "Dr. Grey has gone to visit his grand children. He left me to take care of the town's people. If you will kindly let me check you, I know I can help you feel better."

Gran relaxed and lay back, too sick and tired to fight about it any longer.

Meg waited by the bedroom door until he was done. He worked silently, with the exception of an occasional request for Gran to sit up a little more, or take a deep breath, or roll onto her side. When he was done, he gave her a dose of some medicine in his bag. He stood to leave. "You should be able to sleep now, Mrs. Hollister. Try to rest all you can so you can get better."

Gran's eyes were already growing heavy, whether from the medicine or from the exertion of her check-up, Meg didn't know.

"Is it influenza?" Meg asked as soon as they were in the hallway with the bedroom door closed. Her voice shook with worry and exhaustion

"I don't know yet. It could just be a simple infection. I'll give you a prescription to fill as soon as the pharmacy opens. I will also need to check on her several times in the next few days. My suspicion is that it's a fall cold that has gotten bad. I hope it isn't pneumonia, but only time will tell."

Meg sank with relief against the wall. "I hope with all my heart you are right," she sighed.

"The medicine should help her sleep. You should try to get some sleep while she does." the doctor ordered. "Instead of having you run for the prescription, I'll send someone with it a little later. That way you can stay with her. We can't have you getting sick, too."

Meg nodded. She could barely keep her eyes open as it was. "I'd be happy to try to sleep, believe me," she said with a small laugh.

Meg slept on the floor in Gran's room that morning, so she could hear if Gran called her or tried to get up. Someone from the pharmacy brought the medicine around lunchtime. Dr. Coburg visited again later that evening. Gran's fever was still high, but she was more coherent than she had been earlier in the day.

Two days later, after faithfully taking the medicine, and several visits from the doctor, Gran had improved. On the third day, in the evening, Dr. Coburg pronounced her "on the mend" as he left her room. Gran had fallen asleep on her own, without the help of the medicine for the first time in days.

"Why don't you stay for some soup?" Meg asked as he came into the front room. The delicious smell of it filled the house. "We have fresh bread and apple butter for dessert."

The doctor grinned. "I think I will. It smells delicious."

"How long have you lived with your Gran?" he asked as they ate in the kitchen.

"Only a couple of years," Meg said. "My parents are gone. She needed someone to take care of her. Aunt Elaine had noticed she was getting forgetful. She and Uncle Daniel thought having someone here full time would be a good idea. I needed a place to stay so I came to live here. What made you decide to come to our little town?"

"My father and Dr. Grey are college friends. I'd finished my residency and wanted to go somewhere to learn private practice. Dr. Grey offered to help me learn it here."

"Do you miss the city?" she asked, not knowing how anyone could prefer a city to a village like Hollis.

He grinned at her. "Not a bit! My mother is quite the socialite. She would attend some social function or other several nights a week. She dragged me in as often as possible. No, here it is quiet most evenings. A man can finish a thought in a town like this."

"Has your practice here picked up? I know we've been keeping you busy the last few days. But before that. Were folks accepting you?"

"It's been slow. I expect to see more patients with winter coming on and the influenza outbreak growing worse. I do go into Walton a couple times a week to help out there. Otherwise, I do a good job of keeping a chair warm in Dr. Grey's office. Your cousin said you two were going into Walton to help out as well. How is that going?"

Meg smiled. "We've been working hard. Sometimes it doesn't feel like we're doing much, but I know it is helping. Maybe sometime I'll even be able to get around and see some of the wards in the hospital." She chuckled. Then she grew serious. "Though to hear the nurses talk, it isn't easy to care for the patients these days. We have so many sick from around here, and soldiers coming in from the front needing treatment. There isn't room or staff enough for them all. They look at it as their part to help in the war. That's how Nellie and I see it, too. We couldn't go to France to fight, but we can help those who have."

Dr. Coburg left that evening with the promise that he would come again in a couple of days, but sooner if she needed him. He also assured her that Gran should be fine. It might take a couple weeks for her to convalesce, but she should make a full recovery.

Meg slept well that night for the first time in over a week. As she drifted off, she thought about how much she'd enjoyed sitting and talking with Dr. Coburg. He was handsome. But more than that, he was kind and thoughtful. She sighed and tried not to let herself think of him too much. And she didn't succeed one bit in that endeavor.

Chapter Eleven

It seemed odd that Meg hadn't heard from either Aunt Elaine or Nellie since Gran had been sick. She'd assumed they were going on with their lives as usual, but Aunt Elaine was always so worried about Gran. Meg decided to give it a day or two, then check on them. Gran still needed near constant care, so Meg couldn't spare the time away to see them,

It seemed even more odd to her that, two days later, Dr. Coburg didn't come to check on Gran as he had promised. Not that he needed to. Gran was still weak and preferred sitting up in bed to getting out and sitting in her easy chair. Her fever only came back at night. She was starting to eat. Meg was happy to fix whatever food tempted Gran and she offered it regularly.

There were hours during the day when Gran was resting. Once the fever broke she was able to sleep for long periods of time undisturbed and it helped her improve faster than anything else. But Meg had grown accustomed to being at the hospital three days a week, so filling those long hours at home alone was difficult. She cleaned and washed the laundry and worked on her sewing, but sometimes she just sat and watched over Gran or took a nap herself.

The morning of the third day dawned clear and cold, the coldest morning so far this season. Meg's hands were so cold that she struggled to light a fire in the kitchen stove. Abandoning that endeavor, Met lit a fire in the stone fireplace in the front room. Little by little, the rest of the house warmed.

Once her hands weren't so cold, the fire in the kitchen didn't take long to light. Soon the kitchen was toasty warm from the little black stove. While the coffee boiled, Meg got a tray together to take to Gran in her room.

A knock on the front door interrupted her work. She moved the coffee to a cooler place on the stove and went to answer. Dr. Coburg stood on the front walk looking very tired and very cold.

"Please, please come in!" Meg exclaimed, stepping out of the way.

"I don't dare do that. Your Aunt asked me to come with a message. I also thought I should explain why I didn't check on Mrs. Hollister last night. Nellie has influenza. She's been sick for a couple days, but they didn't call me until yesterday morning. You both must stay away from there. I won't come in and expose you." His eyes were so tired, so concerned. "It's the first case of the season that I know of here. I'm afraid what it will do."

"Can I at least send some warm bread with you? Or some coffee? Are you going back or going home to sleep?" Though she was concerned for the doctor and Nellie, Meg kept her distance.

"I've done all I can right now. I'm going home to sleep. Dr. Grey will be back tomorrow so contact him if you need anything. Is your grandmother doing alright?"

"I'm perfectly alright." Gran's voice came from behind Meg. Then she went into a fit of coughing from the cold air.

"Gran! You need to get back inside so you don't get sick again!" Meg exclaimed.

"You go take care of your grandmother," Dr. Coburg said, turning away.

"And you go take care of yourself," Meg replied her voice filled with concern. He walked away with a wave toward them. Meg waved back, then closed the warmth back into the house.

"I hope he doesn't catch it!" exclaimed Gran. "That influenza is terrible stuff. It would be a shame for this town to lose a good doctor!"

Meg smiled to herself at Gran's words. This, coming from the lady who hadn't wanted to see another doctor besides Dr. Grey only a few days ago.

"He'll be back. I'm sure of that," Gran said with a wink at Meg and patted her arm. She shakily turned toward the front room. "It will be warmer in the front room so I think I'll have my coffee in here like usual. Won't it be nice to do something normal again?"

Dr. Grey called the next afternoon. He was pleased to see Gran up and about. She was still weak and had a bad cough, but she improved daily. She'd been sitting in her chair by the front room window. Once she'd even eaten in the kitchen.

The news from around the village about the influenza wasn't as good. The outbreak was as bad as it had been in the past. Many people had fallen ill. Sadly, this time most of them were young people that seemed in the best of health – like Nellie.

"I'm going to the hospital in town as often as I can," Dr. Grey informed them. "It's even worse there. All the beds are full. They've brought in military cots to make up the difference. It's all they can do to keep up. Boston has turned away transport ships of soldiers and they are sending them up here. They should arrive at any time. When your grandmother is well enough, I know they would appreciate your help once more," he finished, turning to look at Meg.

"I don't know how I'd get there," Meg said. "I can't ask Aunt Elaine to leave Nellie to take me."

"I'd be happy for you to ride with me. My wife will be going as well. They need every available person who is willing."

"Dr. Coburg has been very attentive to your granddaughter." Dr. Grey went on. "I'm a little afraid for his health. It's his first serious case in practice. He seems quite afraid of losing her. There is nothing more he can do, but he checks on her several times a day. It also seems as though some of the Stuart children are coming down with the influenza. We may need to set up a ward here in town."

Dr. Grey and Gran continued to chat, the topic moving to Dr. Grey's visit with his daughter. Meg slipped away to the kitchen with the excuse of making tea for everyone on this cold day. She needed to be alone.

The news of Dr. Coburg being so attentive to Nellie didn't surprise her, but it also pained her. She'd been silly to even imagine that he would be interested in her when there was the beautiful Nellie to consider. Nellie, who even in sickness managed to maintain a lovely presence. Their talk the other night over soup had been so homey, so friendly, so pleasant. But that was all it was — a visit between friends. She had hoped for more but that's all there was to it as far as Dr. Coburg was concerned.

Chapter Twelve

Later that week, Gran deemed herself "well" and insisted Meg go with Dr. Grey to the hospital in Walton. Word reached them that Nellie had taken a turn for the better and was improving. But it would be weeks before she was well enough to do anything like volunteering.

Monday morning, bright and early, Dr. Grey pulled up in front of Gran's house with his wife and the three of them set off. It seemed like forever since Meg had ridden along this road. She found herself looking for the first glimpse of the ocean and anticipating the saltiness in the air as though this was her first trip to Walton.

Dr. Grey left Meg and hurried off to his work, Mrs. Grey hurried off to hers. Meg went in search of Nurse Rogers.

Nurse Rogers was overjoyed to see Meg. She looked haggard. Meg wondered when she'd last slept.

Nurse Rogers led Meg into the hospital wards, and came straight to the point. "I hope you are able to handle doing patient care. Every bed is full. We've had to bring in more beds. Many nurses are out sick, leaving more for those of us who are well."

The memory of the illness that had killed her parents washed over her. She'd been very sick with it herself, but had recovered after a few weeks. She swallowed down the emotion and met Nurse Rogers' gaze. Her voice was steady when she spoke. "I'm happy to help wherever I'm needed. I'm a fast learner, if there's something I need to know and don't."

"Good. Come with me. How are you with children?"

∞

Meg had no time to think that day. She had never seen anything this bad. The rooms smelled of sickness, human waste, soap, and feverish bodies. Barking coughs rang out over and over around the room. Bed after bed after bed held children of many ages. Some had parents with them, many did not. At least fifty children filled a room meant to house 30, their beds pressed one against another.

Meg moved from one child to the next. She soothed fevered foreheads with cool cloths. Some had to be settled back into bed. As they needed assistance she would get a nurse to help out. One little girl sobbed uncontrollably, begging for her mother. Meg held the girl close and let her cry until she fell into a restless sleep. A nurse took her aside. "Her mother died yesterday," she said in a whisper.

Meg choked on her own tears, memories flooding back that she had to stifle so she could go back to the room and care for the children. The nurse squeezed her arm and moved back into the room as well. Orderlies and volunteers brought lunch to the room for those well enough to eat, but most were too weak to feed themselves so Meg moved from bed to bed, spoon feeding those who needed to eat, but could not help themselves.

She was so tired that night that she could barely move. The drive home with the Greys was silent. When she got home, Meg bathed in their tiny bathtub and put her dress in water and soap to soak. Then she collapsed into a kitchen chair and sat for a long time. Gran continued stirring the beans on the stove in silence.

After a difficult battle with her emotions, Meg began to cry. Gran came over and put her arm around Meg's shoulders and let her sob into her hands. She patted and soothed, just like Meg had been doing all day to those children. Then she offered a handkerchief so Meg could wipe the tears.

"Do you need to talk about it?" Gran asked when Meg was able to talk again.

"So many children are sick. It brought back memories I was hoping to never think about again." The tears came again as Meg tried to talk. "A little girl was there who was begging for her mom, but her mom had died." This time she did sob, even harder than before.

"I'm glad you are helping," Gran said. "It will help you heal. You are strong, Meg. Stronger than many girls your age. But you shouldn't have to bear this without pain. Embrace the pain. It will make you even stronger, more compassionate."

"It's too hard, Gran. I can't go back." Meg hiccuped through her tears.

"You can go back. I know you will. You can give those children sympathy they won't get from anyone else." Gran smiled and patted her again, a tear of her own sliding down her cheek. She brushed it away and moved back to the stove. "Now. Supper is ready. Would you get the plates, please?"

No matter how tired she was, Meg had a hard time going to sleep that night. The day played over and over in her head. Meg finally fell into a restless sleep, full of strange dreams. She woke wondering if sleep had done any good at all.

Chapter Thirteen

Jack hated the ocean. He hated being on this infernal boat. He hated being in pain and having to listen to the moans of pain from those around him. He hated everything.

Upon his arrival in London, he'd been taken to a hospital and evaluated. A doctor stood over him and stared at the burns on his legs. He poked the tissue and prodded. Jack stifled back cries of pain as best he could.

"This man needs to be bandaged. Why hasn't he been bandaged before now?" the doctor asked the orderly standing nearby.

The orderly shrugged. "Procedure on the front is to leave the burns open until they close on their own."

"Bandage his legs. We'll watch him for a couple days. He can go on the next ship to America." The doctor turned to the patient in the next bed, Jack and his pain forgotten.

Now, on the ship to the states, Jack had bandage changes to look forward to twice a day. They were excruciating. They saturated the bandages with water and waited for the yellow discharge to soften. Then they removed the bandages. It felt like they were ripping every inch of scar tissue and muscle off his legs every time. Once they were finished, they'd smear a salve of some sort on his legs and re-bandage them. The salve burned as it entered the now open wounds. It smelled antiseptic. Jack began to associate the smell with pain.

Sometimes, before treating him they would hold a rag soaked in ether in front of his nose. At first it helped. The ether allowed him to drift away from the pain in his legs. He felt like he was floating above his body, watching the whole process. Eventually, he built up tolerance to it and it stopped working. He'd close his eyes, as though the ether had worked and focus on something else.

Jack avoided everyone on the ship. Why make friends when they'd probably just die? He couldn't eat. The constant rocking of the boat and subsequent seasickness made sure of that. He rarely slept. He lay awake at night and daydreamed of home.

They'd have finished harvesting. Mom would be stripping the trees of the last of the apples and putting those away for the winter. Dad would be patching things around the farmyard in preparation for cold weather and winter storms. They'd be harvesting the last of the vegetables, potatoes, and gourds.

What would they think of their son who could no longer walk, who wouldn't be able to help them around the farm any more?

Jack didn't fight the dark thoughts that overwhelmed him night and day. After being gruffly rebuffed from conversation or any and all distractions, his fellow shipmates and the ever-present orderlies left him alone. The crossing from England back to the United States passed in slow misery.

They reached Boston Harbor one brilliant, warm day in late October. Jack allowed himself to be pushed out onto the deck into the sunshine for the first time in weeks. He squinted at the buildings in the distance. The ship turned north and Boston faded into the distance. Two days later, they docked in Maine.

Those who were well enough were escorted to the train station and given discharge papers and tickets home. Jack watched these men with disinterest. Many had injuries that had already healed. They'd never be the men they had been before. War and injury had seen to that. But they'd be back with their families. Families who didn't understand what they'd seen or experienced. Jack sighed, relieved he didn't have to see his family yet. At the same time, he longed for home.

Ambulances met the ship, prepared to carry the injured to nearby hospitals. Little by little, the men were carried or pushed off the boat onto the docks. Jack wanted to fall out of the chair and kiss the ground. To his horror, his world continued to rock as if he'd never left the ship.

An orderly pushed him to an ambulance along with several other men he didn't know. A nurse in a stiff blue dress and white apron met them, along with another orderly from the hospital.

"That's the last of them?" the nurse questioned, looking at a clipboard and ticking names off one by one.

"For now, yes. They might send a couple more up by special ambulance once they stabilize enough to be taken off the ship."

The nurse gave Jack a look up and down. "Can't this one get into the ambulance on his own?"

"He can't walk. Burns on his legs and feet."

"Ah. Well then, get him inside so we can be off. We have a drive ahead of us and a bad fever outbreak waiting for us when we get back."

The orderly behind Jack raised his brows. "We avoided several other ports because of the fever."

"You can't avoid the fever these days. It's everywhere. All you can do is hope you don't catch it."

The two orderlies lifted Jack out of the wheelchair and into the ambulance. The nurse stepped up behind him and settled herself at the back. The orderlies shut them inside. A moment later the engine revved to life and they began rattling their way down the road.

"You just as well make yourself comfortable," said the nurse. Following her own advice, she settled into her seat, leaned her head back and closed her eyes.

∞

Jack hadn't meant to close his eyes, but the rocking of the ambulance, so like the rocking of the ship, had lulled him to sleep. He didn't know how long he'd been out. They were pulling into a town, not unlike his hometown back in Indiana. For one, blissful moment, his mind tricked him into believing that's where they were. He blinked. They passed a building with "Walton Hardware" painted across the top and the daydream came tumbling down around him.

The ambulance pulled to a stop in front of a tall brick building near the middle of town. The engine cut out, and a moment later, the orderly appeared at the back of the ambulance and opened the door. The nurse clambered down first and hurried inside. A moment later she was back with a wheelchair.

"Too bad you can't help me get you out of here," the orderly grunted as he reached for Jack and lifted him out of the ambulance into the chair. "Good thing you're so skinny or I wouldn't be able to do this."

Shame covered Jack's face. He looked at his lap and wouldn't look up, not even to see where they were taking him in the hospital. They pushed him into a ward full of men. The ward was so full, in fact, that most of the beds didn't have enough space around them for someone to walk.

The orderly pushed him to the last bed in the room, one with a curtain partial obscuring it, and lifted Jack out of the chair and onto the bed. He left without another word. Jack settled himself on the bed as best as he could and relaxed. For the first time in weeks, he wasn't rocking. The motion sickness slowly ebbed away, replace by intense fatigue. Within minutes, Jack had fallen asleep again.

Days passed, flowing into one another with no differences significant enough for Jack to mark the passage of time. Sick men were brought into the room. Those well enough to do so, left. Doctors came and changed his bandages. The ether they gave him did nothing. He tried not to thrash around, but now and then he couldn't stop a moan from escaping.

At least the food here was marginally better than the food had been on his trip home. Or maybe it was the fact that he was stationary, and didn't fear he'd throw it all up again. Whatever it was, he found he could eat, if only a little. But after days of the same foods every morning, noon, and evening, he struggled to stomach any of it and stopped eating again.

One afternoon, the pain in his legs was the worst it had been for days. He dreaded the impending dressing change. They were understaffed and the doctor rushed to get him finished and move on to the next patient. Jack groaned when he saw them bring in the supplies they would need for his legs that afternoon. He watched the doctor turn to the matron and speak in hushed tones. She nodded and left.

And orderly stepped closer to Jack's bed and held out the rag with ether toward his nose. Jack shook his head. The fumes did nothing but give him a headache.

The doctor gave Jack and the orderly a forced smile. "Shall we begin?"

Chapter Fourteen

The long days of volunteering did not get any easier for Meg, but she put her head down and worked. She felt stronger after her talk with Gran. Better able to handle whatever she had to deal with.

There were more children in the ward each day. Meg didn't know how they'd managed to press any more beds into the space. Some, from the days before, had improved, but most were still very sick.

She had a special place in her heart for the little girl who had lost her mother. She checked on the child each time she went past the bed. The girl was almost delirious with fever, moaning and thrashing around on her bed. Her father shuffled in to see her one afternoon, pale and looking unwell himself, but desperate to be with his little girl.

Day after day followed the same pattern. Meg began to steel herself for the pain the next day might bring. How many more sick children would she find in the ward? How many of those who were already sick would die? Meg wished she could go back to making bandages. At the same time, Meg found healing as she cared for the sick. She began to see the blessing left by the illness that had taken her parents. As time passed and others of the hospital staff fell ill, Meg toiled on, without catching this horrible sickness that targeted the otherwise young and healthy around her.

Nurse Rogers came for her one afternoon. With assurances from the nurses on duty that they could spare her, Nurse Rogers led Meg to a section of the hospital that she hadn't visited since her tour the first day, several months ago.

"A new group of soldiers arrived last week. We have so many sick right now that we don't have the staff to properly care for them. Some of these men are the worst cases I've seen from the front so far. How is your stomach? Can you handle the sight of blood and other bodily fluids?" Nurse Rogers stopped at a bed separated from the rest by curtained dividers and turned to Meg to ask the question.

"Yes, I think so. I suppose so. I've never tried," she replied, hesitating.

"You won't faint." It was more a statement of fact from Nurse Rogers than a question.

"Oh, no! Of course not! I've never fainted before in my life. I don't intend to start now." Meg was emphatic.

Nurse Rogers moved one of the dividers and stepped inside. Meg followed. An orderly and a doctor were already there working over an unconscious man. He was wrapped from his hips to his feet in bandages. The bandages were covered in yellowish blood. She fought the urge to gag at the offensive odor as she stepped into the small space.

"They are changing his bandages. The doctor gave him ether to make him sleep, but he is still moving around too much. He's moving so much they can't work on him. I don't think he is aware of what is going on. He's never fought during a bandage change before. They need you to stand at his head and make sure he is breathing. Check his pulse now and then to make sure it doesn't drop too low. Here," and she showed Meg where to place her fingers to check. "If he wakes up let them know. Changing the bandages is too much pain for him to handle awake. Even asleep these men moan and move about. If he wakes, you might have to help hold him down while they work."

She turned to leave, then stopped and looked at the doctor in charge. "This girl has been invaluable to us in the last weeks. She knows how to handle herself. You can focus on your job. You don't have to worry about her."

Meg felt the pleasure of that high praise and steeled herself, determined to help no matter how difficult. She turned to the man lying in front of her on the bed.

He was pale with sandy brown hair and a smattering of freckles across his face. He was so thin his bones showed in a disturbing way as he lay there. She could tell he had once been a strong, muscular man.

As the doctor and his aides began working Meg had to concentrate so the sounds they were making wouldn't make her ill. But it was the smell – blood and bodily fluids, combined with whatever medicine they had smeared on the wounds – that was most difficult to deal with. The thought of Nurse Rogers' compliment helped her keep focus and not be sick. She kept her eyes on his face, making sure there was a distinct rise and fall of his chest. She took his pulse. It was fast but steady.

One bandage was off. Out of the corner of her eye, she could see his leg and it horrified her. Involuntarily, her eyes pulled to the sight. His leg didn't look human anymore. It looked like his skin had been burned completely away and in its place was scar tissue, twisting, angry red, and oozing yellow fluid. The doctor snipped at the edges of this scar tissue. She though she might be able to see muscle under it. He was missing some toes on his foot. She quickly looked back at his face, checked his pulse, checked his breathing, the sight of his wounds still imprinted in her mind's eye.

His eyes fluttered, then opened. Meg started to look up to gesture to the doctor that the patient was awake. The young man blinked once or twice and shook his head. Then he winced in pain.

Jack had never been through a dressing change this difficult. He felt like he couldn't fight any more. He couldn't fight the pain, the despair, the memories.

They expected him to sleep after the ether so he closed his eyes and thought about home, just as he had done so many times before. He thought of the apple and pumpkin pies his mother would be making this time of year. He thought of the warm days and crisp nights. He thought of the frost covering the ground and the hot coffee he and his father would drink first thing after they finished milking.

Instead of calming him, the thoughts increased his pain. In addition to the agony in his legs, he felt like his heart was breaking. Broken heart, broken body. All he needed was a broken mind. Maybe he already had it and didn't know.

The doctor had reached the final layer and had begun to remove it. They'd moistened the bandages to aid in their removal, but it didn't seem to help today. He moaned and twitched away from the doctor involuntarily. He shouldn't be able to move his legs but they could move on their own, without his control.

"Looks like we've got nerve endings growing back," murmured the doctor to the orderly. "Hold him down."

"I am, sir," the orderly said through gritted teeth.

Jack tried to take some deep breaths. He couldn't breathe. He gasped in air and tried to force it back out but couldn't. The doctor removed more bandage. Jack cried out.

"Give him more ether. He's not out," said the doctor. He returned to his work.

But Jack had mercifully passed out.

He came to, and found he had not missed enough of the dressing change. They still weren't done. Something was different. Small hands rested on his wrist. The doctor removed part of the bandage and he heard a soft, feminine gasp.

Jack opened his eyes and saw an angel standing above him. He blinked. No, not an angel, just a lovely woman who studied his face with concern.

A soft moan escaped his lips, but he closed his eyes when the doctor looked up.

68

"Do we need more ether? I'm pretty sure we've given him all we can for now. I can't imagine the pain he is in for him to be moaning when he is knocked out." The doctor turned back to the miserable job in front of him.

The last of the bandages were off. They washed the wounds. Then they slathered the salve on them once more and began wrapping them again. Jack closed his eyes and wished he could pass out again.

$$\infty$$

The man on the bed moved his head back and forth. Moans and groans of agony wrenched from him.

Meg didn't bother to check his pulse. He was obviously awake even while pretending not to be. She placed both hands on his skeletal shoulders to try to keep him from moving too much.

"He's awake, isn't he?" the orderly asked.

Meg nodded without a word. She hoped with all her heart that the man would be okay once they finished changing the bandages.

What seemed like hours passed, but it was only a few minutes until they were done. The doctor washed in the the basin on the table, then left the room. The orderly cleaned up the mess and removed the dirty sheet from under the man's bandaged legs.

Meg started to leave, but the man reached out and gripped her arm.

"Wait." His eyes, now open, held hers.

Jack had watched this angel. She hadn't flinched away from the sight of his legs. Once she'd seen them, she hadn't looked at him with disgust or pity. He hadn't anticipated this reaction from anyone, let alone a beautiful woman like her.

She waited while the orderly finished. Once he was gone, she brought pillows that were laying on the side table and placed them behind his back to prop him up.

"That's better." He sighed with relief once he was settled. "Thank you for staying. I need something to keep my mind off the pain for a little while. Can you chat for a few minutes?"

"I'd love to." Meg smiled. She perched on the edge of his bed. "I'm Meg Hollister. I volunteer here at the hospital several days a week."

"My name is Jack Collins. Fresh back on American soil from France. It's good to see American faces and hear American accents again." He tried a pained smile, then grimaced and tried to shift on the bed. But no position was any more comfortable than another. He fell back against the pillows.

"If you don't mind my asking, what happened to you?" Meg asked. "You don't have to talk about it if it is too hard. We've heard some awful stories from over there." She frowned at the memories.

"Mustard gas." he stated simply. "I was in a battle and jumped into a trench. I don't know where I was when the gas got me, but it did. I know guys who died of it. Terrible way to go. A bullet would be better. Less painful." Jack winced against the pain and the despair. "Kind of wish I could have joined them. How one goes on living with pain like this I don't know. As it is, I'm not sure I could stand being on these stumps of legs for any amount of time. They looked worse before, but they still look pretty awful."

"I saw," Meg said.

"You've got more guts than most of the girls I know." He shook his head and looked at her with admiration. "They keep telling me they are healing. It seems crazy to hear that, but still feel so much pain and not be able to use them."

Jack fell silent. He stared off into the distance. Meg waited for him to come back from his thoughts. When he did, he changed the subject. "So, are you a nurse? Do you live around here?"

"No, I'm not a nurse," Meg replied with a smile. "I live in a town not far from here and come up here to help out. My cousin and I made those lovely bandages you are now wearing on your legs, among other things." She smiled and pointed at his legs. "But lately

70

I've been helping out in the children's ward. This place is full to capacity."

"You help with influenza patients?" He was surprised. "How is it you don't get sick?"

"I don't really know," she said. "I did have something a couple years ago. Maybe I'm immune. I've been around it enough for the last few weeks that I should have gotten it."

Nurse Rogers came to the opening of the curtains and looked in. "Dr. Grey is looking for you. He is in the lobby. I see you both survived the ordeal." She smiled and left.

"You'll come again to visit, won't you?" Jack pleaded. He wanted to see her again. Needed to see her. He reached out and caught her hand.

"Plan for it." Meg said with a smile. She squeezed his fingers, then turned and left the small space.

Chapter Fifteen

Meg visited Nellie that Saturday. She was sitting up in their front room swathed in blankets, with her feet resting on an ottoman. Aunt Elaine had her sipping tea. She looked thin after her illness – far thinner than she should be. But the glow was coming back to her fair cheeks. She didn't seem as frail as Meg remembered being after she'd been sick two years ago.

"Here's some bread and some of that wonderful apple preserves Gran makes. She said it would fatten you right up again." Meg said with a grin and both girls laughed at the thought.

"How are you feeling?" Meg asked.

"I'm feeling so much better!" Nellie enthused. "There were days there when I was pretty sure I was dying. But of course Philip was here to make sure I didn't." She gave Meg a coy smile and went on. "Philip almost never left my side the whole time. It was so reassuring to have him here. He is such a good doctor!"

Here it came. The deluge of information about the wonderful relationship she had with the town's young doctor. Meg sat and listened to every detail that Nellie could remember for the next forty-five minutes. He'd brought the medicine himself and insisted on giving it to her to make sure she received the correct dosage. He sat with her during the day so Aunt Elaine could sleep. He'd been coming since she'd gotten better to make sure she didn't relapse or do anything she shouldn't do. He sat and read to her. They talked. She knew all about his family, his mother and sisters, his father's business. Nellie didn't seem to notice whether or not Meg responded at all.

"So I think I can safely say we're becoming great friends," Nellie finally finished. "He insists I call him Philip since there isn't a large gap in our ages. Mom wasn't keen on the idea but she's warmed to it."

"Now," Nellie went on, changing the subject, "tell me about the hospital. Philip said you've been going again and that it is busy there."

Meg smiled. She didn't know how much Nellie really wanted to hear. So she kept it short.

"You aren't the only one sick with the influenza. It looks like this outbreak is far worse than the outbreak earlier this year. There are so many people in the hospital right now that they don't have any more beds. I've been helping with the children. There isn't much anyone can do to make them feel better. Sometimes a gentle hand and reassurance is all they need."

"You are far better at that than I am," Nellie said with a resigned sigh. "Philip says I can't go back for at least another month. Who knows, by that time they might not even need me anymore. I'm not very good around sick people. Oh, did I tell you about when Philip brought his butterfly specimens over the other day?" And Nellie launched into another story about herself and Philip.

"If she hadn't been so thin and pathetic looking I would have gotten up and left right then." Meg said when she told Gran about the whole ordeal that evening. She sighed. "I don't know why I tolerate her. She can be so self-centered and egotistical."

"She was raised to be that way," Gran said with a click of her tongue and a shake of her head. "Nothing good is going to come of her throwing herself at this young doctor."

Chapter Sixteen

After the weekend away from the hospital Meg was eager to get back and see the children. Several had improved enough to go home. She was happy for them, but missed getting to say goodbye. The little girl whose mother had died was there, improved, but still weak. Meg brought some books with her from home and read to the children. The children who were well enough gathered around to see the pictures. The rest lay in bed and listened.

Other times, while caring for the worst of the sick children she would tell stories to all those near enough to listen. One afternoon, they played a game where she started a story and each child took a turn adding to it. They liked that one so much they begged for it every day.

Word of how well she handled the bandage change got around to the nurses. Sometimes she was called to help with that ordeal for soldiers other than Jack. She never got over how awful it was. Some of the men were worse than others. They all needed someone to distract them when the doctors were removing the bandages, applying the medicine, and cleaning the wounds.

"Why do we have so many burned soldiers? What about all the other wounded?" she asked Nurse Rogers one day. The poor man whose dressing they had changed was finally sleeping.

"Most of the other wounds heal more quickly. By the time we get them, they've been in a field hospital in England or France for a while. The ones with the worst wounds have died. The ones with the least have healed and gone home. There were many soldiers on that boat that were on their way home to finish healing. These here are well enough to travel back to America, but not well enough to go home. They still need constant care. They were moved here to free up space there for others."

Each day, before Dr. Grey was ready to leave, Meg hurried to Jack's bedside for a short visit. She brought a book to read to him, if he wanted. She brought poetry and short stories. At first, there were days he didn't seem to notice what she read to him. He'd stare into the distance with vacant eyes, occasionally wincing in pain.

One afternoon, he asked her to leave the book of Robert Frost poems she'd brought. His request surprised her. She didn't think he'd been listening. She placed the book on the bed where he could reach it, then slid her fingers into his and squeezed. He met her eyes and squeezed her fingers in return. Then he gave her a sad smile and looked away once more.

Sometimes he wanted to talk. Or, rather, he'd ask Meg questions and listen to her answers. He asked her about how many people were sick, what she'd been doing all day.

When he asked her what she'd done the previous weekend, Meg told him that she'd visited Nellie.

"I'm sure she enjoyed your company," he said. "It certainly helps the time pass more quickly for me." Jack smiled at her, a rare treat. It still didn't reach his eyes.

Meg smiled back at him. "Is it that bad the rest of the time?"

He sighed. "Sometimes I don't see anyone all day except the nurses."

Meg cocked an eyebrow. "You could talk to the men around you. I'm sure they'd all love some conversation, too. You could take turns around reading. I'm happy to bring more books."

Jack gave her another sad smile and shook his head. "It's not that easy. Now, tell me about your visit to your cousin."

"There isn't much to tell. My cousin irritates me. She seemed glad to see me, but then she spent the whole visit talking about this man she's been trying to catch for the last few weeks. He's her doctor, single, very good looking. I guess I don't blame her. But I don't want to hear about it every time we're together."

"Are you jealous?"

Meg met Jack's gaze. His eyes searched hers, a flicker of light there for the first time. He needed the truth, deserved the truth. He cared whether she was jealous of Nellie or not.

"A few weeks ago I was. I thought the doctor was interested in me, but was mistaken. I guess deep down I'm jealous she has a beau and I don't. She's beautiful. I shouldn't be surprised he likes Nellie."

"If he is her beau and it isn't all in her imagination."

"I don't understand," Meg said, puzzled.

"Maybe he's leading her on. Some men feel powerful when they have beautiful women falling all over them. Maybe he was leading you on, too."

"I doubt it," she said. Then she laughed and looked down at her hands, embarrassed. "I can't believe I'm dumping all this on you. You barely know me! Thanks for listening." Meg looked up at Jack.

Jack's eyes drooped shut.

"I'll see you tomorrow, Jack. You rest and get better." Meg reached out and squeezed Jack's fingers like she always did. He gave her a sleepy smile and squeezed back.

Gran liked hearing about Jack. She asked Meg about him every evening and murmured things like "poor man!" and "that dear boy" the whole time.

The next morning she sent a pound cake with Meg. "Tell him to eat the whole thing. I knew a boy that was burned when I was a girl. His doctor swore that eating eggs would make him get better faster. That cake has nine eggs in it, so it should help him heal. Tell him if he is well enough by Christmas we want him to come visit for the day. It will give him something to look forward to."

Meg didn't know about that. Would they even let the soldiers leave the hospital? She asked Dr. Grey about it as they drove to Walton that morning.

"Gran suggested having a soldier come for Christmas. Do they let them do that?" she asked.

"They do, if the man is well enough to move about on his own and doesn't need constant supervision. Do you have someone in mind?" He glanced over his shoulder at her with a quizzical look.

"I've befriended a man named Jack Collins. But I don't know if he'd be able to come. I don't think he can even get out of bed. He told me he might not ever walk again."

"I know the man." Dr. Grey nodded. "His doctor doesn't see any reason why he shouldn't be able to walk. In fact, he told me last week his wounds were improving. Poor man has decided he can't walk. There is no telling what these men have experienced and seen. Going to your Gran's for Christmas might be just the thing he needs. You should ask him. See what some hope can do. If he has the hope of not having to be in that bed over Christmas, of being with a family, maybe he'll give it a try."

"There is some question about how we'd get him from there to our house," Meg said. "But we have time to figure that out."

"I'm sure someone will be glad to help," Dr. Grey said with a little wink her direction.

The day seemed to drag despite being as busy as normal. Instead of taking a lunch break in the dining room Meg went to visit Jack. He looked surprised, but not disappointed to see her so early in the afternoon.

"I brought a gift from my grandmother. It's her special pound cake. She said it would help you heal faster, and that you were to eat the whole thing." Meg produced the cake, tucked into a tin, and brought it to his bedside table. The remainders of his lunch were sitting there virtually untouched.

He smiled sheepishly as she looked from him to the lunch. "Did you eat anything at all?" she asked, horrified at how little had been taken from the plate.

"It doesn't appeal to me. I guess it *is* food and it nourishes. The pain makes me sick to my stomach. I don't feel like eating most of the time."

"You have to eat," Meg said. She set the tin down, lifted the lid, and, using the knife from his tray, cut him a large slice. "Try this and see if you don't get an appetite for more." It smelled so good Meg took a thin slice for herself. "Gran is going to ask if you ate it all. If I eat more than this I can't tell her you did."

He took a bite, and then another. "It *is* good. The best food I've had in a long time. Kind of tastes like a cake my Mom makes." The piece was gone in a few more bites. She cut him another and then settled on the side of his bed.

"How would you like to have as much of my Gran's good food as you can eat?" she asked. "You're invited to spend Christmas with us. I wasn't sure if they would let you. But it turns out that if you are well enough to get around on your own, even with a wheelchair, they will let you come. What do you think?"

"That would be wonderful." His eyes brightened. He straightened in the bed. For the first time he smiled. Not the cynical smile made only by his lips, but a smile that reached all the way to his eyes. "Are you serious that they would let me?" Then his face fell. "You've seen my legs. You know I can't walk."

"The doctor told me if you work on it, you could get back the use of your legs. It will be hard work, but you can do it. You'll have to take it slowly. Besides, you don't have to be able to walk by Christmas. All you have to do is be able to get out of bed."

He shook his head. "It's only three weeks away. I don't think I can do it."

"I'll help you." Meg was enthusiastic. She wasn't going to let his discouragement dampen her resolve that he'd spend Christmas somewhere other than inside these four walls that smelled of human

78

waste, bodily fluids, and antiseptic. "I know with a little work every day you can do it." She smiled, determined, and squeezed his fingers.

Jack squeezed back and held on. "What if I can't?"

"You won't know until you try. Can you at least try?"

"For the promise of real food at Christmas in a place other than a battlefield or hospital? I'll try. For you, I'll try."

The orderly came back for the lunch dishes and Meg stood and moved out of his way. "I've got to get back. You'd better eat every bite of that cake."

The worst of the influenza outbreak was over. The children were all improving and no one new had been admitted for a while. She had a lot of entertaining that needed to be done, but her mind was elsewhere. Her thoughts kept going to a young man in a bed in another part of the hospital. Would he be able to learn to walk well enough to come to their house for Christmas?

Chapter Seventeen

"I don't know if I can do it. The pain is so intense," Jack told Meg the next afternoon when she visited him. The empty cake tin sat beside his bed. He told her he'd made a nurse rinse it off for him and promised he'd eaten every bite of it himself. "You can't imagine how much it hurts. It feels like tearing, ripping, burning pain, and shoots all the way up into my shoulders."

"Is there something I can do to make it easier for you?" Meg asked.

"You can bring me more of that cake," he chuckled.

Meg liked how he looked when he smiled. The way his eyes lit up like he had some secret joke. The way he showed all his teeth. He hadn't smiled like that often, but this was twice in the last two days. She felt like they'd made progress.

"Seriously, though," Jack continued, "I don't know. Maybe if every day you helped me move my legs back and forth that would loosen them up. I asked the doctor last night. He said that I should be able to learn to use them again. He didn't think the damage was so bad. But I'll have to go slow. Last night, I tried to move them, but the scars broke open and bled." He moved the sheet to show her the blood on the bandages.

Meg winced. "You are a stronger person than I am," she said softly. "Gran did send some food for you again. This time it's a piece of apple pie. I'm not sure how it's supposed to help. Maybe we could use it as a reward. If you work to move your legs, you can eat it."

He put his head back on the pillow and laughed. It sounded rusty, like he hadn't done it in a while. "You are ever the optimist. Okay, let's try."

The next few minutes were painful for both of them. Meg was afraid to hurt him. He told her over and over that he couldn't feel her touch his legs because of the bandages and burns. She could hold on to them, and he wouldn't know the difference. As she gently pushed up on his feet to bend his leg at the hip and knee he winced at first, then moaned. She started to put it back, but he stopped her. "No! I have to keep going!" So they did. Up and down and up and down. It wasn't long before Jack was sweating and as pale as the sheet on his bed.

"We have to quit. You've more than earned this pie." Meg handed him the pie in its small dish.

"You'll have to set it on the table. I don't think I can eat it right now," he replied. He lay back on the pillow with his eyes closed. Sweat poured down his face. A few minutes passed in silence.

"Well, that was one of the more difficult things I've ever done," Jack finally said, still breathing hard from his earlier effort. He began to regain his color.

Meg propped him up on his pillows and handed him the pie. Then she settled onto her usual spot on the edge of his bed.

"I found out today they won't be needing me at the hospital every day anymore," Meg said. She watched Jack pick small bites of pie off with the fork she'd brought and chew them slowly.

"That's the saddest news I've had in a long time. What will I do for company?"

"You'll have to get one of the orderlies to come talk to you," Meg said with a chuckle.

"Seriously, Meg. You're keeping me sane. I look forward to your company every day." His eyes told her that he wasn't teasing her.

Meg's laughter faded into a smile. "I'll still be here every other day. I'll bring books for you to read. You could talk to some of your roommates in the meantime. Then, if you work very hard, you'll be able to visit my town, my Gran, my family."

"I'm looking forward to it." Jack set the empty plate aside. "I'm not, however, looking forward to the daily pain I get to endure to get ready."

"You'll get to meet Nellie in a week or two." The thought had just occurred to Meg. It made her nervous to consider Nellie meeting Jack.

"I'm sure it will be great." Jack sagged, exhausted, back onto his pillows. "I can't imagine she will be quite the engaging conversationalist her cousin is."

Meg burst out laughing at his sarcasm. "Oh, hardly! I'm known for my witty repartee.

"Well, I'd better go find Dr. Grey so he doesn't have to wait for me." She collected the plate. "Keep up the hard work."

Jack caught her wrist before she could stand, then slid his hand down to squeeze her fingers. "Thank you," he said quietly, serious again. "You've helped me at least as much or more than any person in this hospital. God sent you to my room that day because He knew I was in desperate need of some hope." He released her hand, but his eyes held hers for a moment longer.

She flushed and fumbled with the plate, not sure what to say. Muttering something dismissive, Meg fled the room.

Jack stared at the ceiling. He couldn't see it. The ward nurse had turned the lights off for the night an hour ago. For the first time in weeks, Jack didn't feel like the darkness of the room was pressing in on him. He shifted around on the bed in an effort to get comfortable and go to sleep.

"You thinking about your pretty young nurse?" came a voice from the bed next to his.

"She's not a nurse," Jack answered automatically.

"She's an angel," came a voice from across the aisle. "A brown haired angel."

Jack smiled in the darkness. Smiling came easily when he thought about Meg. He could see her determined brown eyes looking at him that afternoon. He saw them filled with compassion and tears at his obvious pain. Yet the determination was still there. It was the only way he'd been able to keep going.

"Angels are blonde. Everyone knows that," scoffed the voice next to Jack. "Besides, you got your own brown haired angel back home, Teddy."

"Yes, I do," said the man across the aisle, his voice filled with pride, a grin evident in his voice. "Doc says I'll get to see my brown haired angel for Christmas."

"Yeah, they're telling me I'll be out of here before Christmas, too. My stump is healing up just fine." The man next to Jack was grinning, too. "But I got no angel waiting for me back home. Mom died of the fever earlier this year after I was shipped out."

"Sorry, man," said Teddy. "That's rough."

The men fell silent. Jack shifted on his bed. The springs squeaked. The man next to him shifted, too.

"Who's waiting for you back home?" asked the voice beside him.

"My mom and dad have a farm. Last I heard they were all doing well."

"You got a girl back there?" the man asked. "Cause if you do, I'd love to get to know the beauty that's been visiting you."

"Meg. Her name is Meg." Jack didn't try to keep the annoyance out of his voice. "And no, I don't have anyone waiting for me back home. Not that it's any of your business."

"Yeah, man, sorry." The bed next to him squeaked again as the man turned away.

Jack sighed. "No, I'm the one who should apologize."

"Apology accepted."

Silence fell again. Then the man next to him broke it once more.

"I can *not* stop thinking about real food. My aunts will go all out for Christmas. Turkey or maybe ham, pies, cakes. Real food. Not this slop they call food here or the food we got in that army hospital. Your girl brought that pound cake and I thought I'd died and gone to heaven just smelling it."

Jack chuckled.

"He laughs!" Teddy exclaimed.

Jack shook his head, though he knew the men couldn't see it in the dark. "Not often enough, anymore." He sighed. "The cake was every bit as good as it smelled."

"I wish I had an angel visiting me and bringing me cake," said the voice beside him. "I can't get home quick enough."

Jack finally drifted off, dreaming of pound cake, apple pie, and Christmas that couldn't come soon enough to suit them.

Chapter Eighteen

Jack worked hard those next weeks. After months of disuse his muscles screamed in pain when moved. He had to fight through the pain of the burns and the stiff scar tissue that had formed as his legs healed. Every movement was a painful challenge.

He worked until he could bend both knees and hips. His movements were stiff, awkward, tortured, but he could do it.

Then he worked to sit up and swing his legs over the edge of the bed. They stuck out like wooden sticks, until he could force his knees and hips to relax and bend. Sitting, after lying down for so long, caused waves of dizziness and nausea. He felt like he was going to pass out.

Once he could bend his legs and sit up, Jack found that he could not stand. His legs would not bear his weight after long disuse. He'd try, collapse on the bed, try again. His ankles were weak and he couldn't balance. The week before Christmas he still couldn't stand. Discouragement threatened to overwhelm him.

"I can't do it. I can't stand, let alone walk. You'll have to tell your Gran I can't come." Jack groaned to Meg one afternoon. He'd been fighting to stand up for half an hour, only to feel faint and off balance. Dr. Grey observed the whole ordeal along with Jack's other doctor, Dr. Fulton.

"Standing could be difficult for a while, son," Dr. Fulton stated. "You lost a lot of muscle on your ankles and feet. You're going to have to build that back up again."

"What about crutches or a cane?" Dr. Grey asked. "He can stand as long as he is holding on to something or someone. It could be, given time and use, he'll be able to walk without either. But for now one or the other might be a good idea."

"I'll see what I can find," Dr. Fulton agreed.

Jack sank onto the bed, exhausted. "I should sleep well tonight." He put his head in his hands for a moment. "Wow, am I ever dizzy."

Meg sank onto the bed next to him and rubbed his shoulder. "You are doing well, you know. Two weeks ago you didn't even want to try. You've gone from thinking it was impossible to standing in a very short time.

"Here, Gran sent you cookies. We're baking for Christmas. She wanted you to have these. There will probably be more to come." She handed him a brown paper bag heavy with iced sugar cookies.

Jack pulled out a snowman and took a big bite. He closed his eyes relishing the flavor. "You tell your Gran that her cookies beat out my grandma's any day. Okay, well, maybe not." He attempted a smile. "But she is a great cook."

"I'll tell her," Meg promised. "She'll be happy to know you think so. You've never seen someone so excited about Christmas as she is. You can't give up now, Jack. She'd be so disappointed. Besides, with all the things she's making for you, I'm going to completely lose my figure if you don't come help eat it."

Jack had to laugh. Slowly, painfully, he settled himself back on the bed.

Dr. Fulton examined his legs. They weren't bleeding as badly as they had during the first week, but blood was soaking through the bandages in several places where the scar tissue had torn.

"We'll find you crutches or a cane. If you do go next week you'll need a wheelchair to get to the car. But once you get to their house you're on your own. Dr. Grey said their house isn't large. He thinks that you can get around it without any trouble. Don't give up now. Your progress is remarkable in such a short time."

"Time to head home," Dr. Grey said to Meg. He and Dr. Fulton left the room.

Meg turned back to Jack. "You can do this. I know you can." She gently squeezed his hand where it lay, like the rest of him, exhausted on the bed. He covered her hand with his other one.

"If you say so," Jack replied with a wry grin. "Right now it doesn't feel like it. I'll keep trying for you and your Gran."

Meg squeezed his hand one last time, then stood and left the room. The doctors were deep in conversation in the hall. She walked past them on her way to the front of the hospital. Dr. Fulton followed behind, stopping her.

"You have to know, Miss Hollister, you are the best thing that has happened to that young man in there. Since you came in that day I've seen him go from a man without any inclination to live to a man willing to at least give it a try. There aren't enough words to express my thanks to you. He's a different man today than he was a month ago."

"I was doing what any other decent person would do," said Meg with a shrug. "He's become a good friend. I enjoy spending time with him."

"Thank you for all your help." He shook her hand vigorously.

Meg shrugged again and nodded. His gratitude made her uncomfortable. She'd done nothing special. All she'd done is offer the same comfort and encouragement Gran had given her two years ago. She muttered something about leaving and hurried after Dr. Grey, who had started for the front of the hospital again.

Outside, snow threatened. It was certainly cold enough.

On the way home, she looked out at the ocean like she did every time they drove past. Some days it had been brilliant blue with small white caps. Other times it had been deep teal green with frothy gray foam. Today it was dark gray, almost black with choppy white caps that stood out against the darker color of the water. She saw fishing boats, but she knew they'd probably come back if it got any worse. The ocean calmed her. They turned the bend away from it and into the woods. She lost sight of the ocean. But the rolling waves went on in her imagination. Her mind drifted off onto other things as they rode along in silence, lost in thought and watching the first of the snowflakes fall to the ground.

Chapter Nineteen

The snow was thick and brilliant the next morning when Meg woke up. The blanket over the ground muffled the outdoor sounds. It lent the house a feeling of warmth, even though the temperature had dropped significantly since it stopped snowing.

Meg bounced around her room. The fallen snow made her so happy, almost like a child again. They were supposed to be inside for the day baking Christmas cookies. Maybe, if she hurried, she could get the Stuart girls to go for a romp down the big hill with her.

The coffee smelled wonderful. So did the eggs and ham Gran was frying. Meg hurried into her clothes and tied her hair up in a ribbon. Then she bounded down the stairs to help cook.

The downstairs was cooler than her little upstairs room with the chimney from the living room fireplace going up one wall. Her room had been cool, but the downstairs rooms were cold.

"Why don't you start some cookies so we can get this oven running?" suggested Gran.

Meg was happy to comply. It helped to move around. She mixed the sugar cookies as quickly as possible, but they wouldn't be ready to bake for a while. She set them in the pantry to chill. Then she mixed the snickerdoodles. Those were her personal favorites. Meanwhile, Gran lit the oven.

The eggs and ham were ready and getting cold by this time. Meg waited for the oven to heat and sat and ate her breakfast. The two women lingered over their coffee cups for a few moments, savoring the warmth. Then they went back to work, Gran to wash the dishes and Meg to finish putting cookies on sheets.

"How is your young soldier doing?" Gran asked as she washed.

"Gran," Meg rebuked gently, "He isn't my soldier."

"Of course he is!" Gran exclaimed with a smile. "He's the soldier you look in on at the hospital. It's how I keep it clear in my head."

"Oh, I get it. At the hospital. Versus the soldier I write letters to, or the soldier I see here in town. Gran, please. His family is a long way away. He needs someone to show they care."

"Meg, it's okay to care. It's okay to care because you like him, not just because he's a soldier." It was Gran's turn for gentle rebuke.

"I know, Gran. But he'll heal enough to go home. Most of the soldiers have already. When he does, he'll be a long way from here and we won't be able to see each other. He can't be "my" soldier." The thought made Meg sadder than she cared to admit.

Gran, as usual, had hit on the truth. Often she found herself thinking about Jack, happy to get to spend time with him, enjoying their conversations. She looked forward to them, replayed them in her mind when they weren't together. He needed a friend. For that matter, she did, too. Falling in love with him wasn't a good idea. She needed to be careful, to guard against it. She'd be hurt if he didn't return the feelings.

"Well? You didn't answer my question. How is he doing?" Gran's voice brought her out of her thoughts.

"He is doing well. I've been amazed at the progress he has made over the last couple of days, even. He wants to come for Christmas so badly that he's putting all his effort into walking. His muscles were damaged on his legs and ankles, so he doesn't have strength to stand and balance yet. He'll get it, but it will take longer than we have until Christmas. The doctors are looking for crutches or a cane or something to help him balance." Meg took the first pan of cookies out of the oven. "I'm pretty sure none of these snickerdoodles are making it to those children at the hospital." She laughed and blew on one to cool it enough to taste.

"That's remarkable," Gran said to herself. "It's amazing he could get that far in so short a time."

Meg nodded and pushed the next pan into the oven. "The doctor thinks so, too. He said that Jack is a different man since he gets to do something other than sit in that hospital bed over Christmas. He has new hope. It will be strange to have someone other than family here for Christmas, but I'm excited about it. Oh, he said to tell you that your sugar cookie recipe is almost as good as his grandma's. He loved those cookies you sent."

"You didn't tell him I made them, did you? Like the apple pie you took and claimed I made. Or the pound cake. Meg, he's going to think I'm fattening him up."

"It's better he think that than thinking I'm the one trying to fatten him up. Besides, the man needs some meat on those bones. He's working so hard he's earned it." She grinned at Gran. "I don't care who gets credit for these cookies as long as he eats them. Besides, I told him you sent them, not that you made them."

"Elaine came over yesterday. She said she is planning to start taking you and Nellie to the hospital again. With the fever crisis over, Dr. Grey isn't needed there every day, so he wasn't planning to go very often anymore. I guess Dr. Coburg has taken a place at the hospital and will be moving to Walton. He wants a more secure income than he's had here in town," Gran said. She began rolling and cutting the sugar cookies Meg had mixed earlier.

"I wonder why on earth he could want a more secure income." Meg couldn't keep the sarcasm out of her voice. "Or why Nellie would suddenly be so eager to get back to the hospital now that her beloved doctor works there." She sighed and began mixing up ginger snaps. The whole thing seemed strange to her. A few weeks ago, Dr. Coburg sat in this very kitchen telling Meg how much he enjoyed country life. Meg wondered at the change of heart.

"Why does it still bother you so much?" Gran asked.

"I think I'm just hurt," Meg said.

"You aren't interested in him, too, are you?" Gran asked. "He's a nice man, but if he'll be caught by any old woman who sets her cap for, him then he isn't worth the energy spent worrying about it. The man should be the one doing the chasing and catching, not the girl."

"I'm not interested in him, Gran. At one time I think I could have been with the right encouragement. No, I'm not about to be interested in the same man as Nellie. She'll always win in a situation like that. Maybe that's what hurt. Given the choice, the doctor went after her. I think I'm afraid no man will ever decide to love me, when he could be interested in Nellie."

"That isn't true, Meg. The right man will have eyes only for you. He won't even think about Nellie when she's around. This Jack fellow really likes you. So see, not every man is after Nellie." Gran was trying to be encouraging.

"He doesn't 'like' me, Gran. And he's never even met Nellie. He will at Christmas. I'm scared about that. If I don't let myself be interested in him, then if he decides he likes her better, it won't hurt so much. But it will hurt. It's too late for that."

"Don't worry about it, love. Things will all work out the way they are supposed to. You'll see." Gran's tone was soothing. She sounded confident. Meg had to smile, even if she didn't quite believe her.

"Aunt Elaine is worried about it," Gran went on. "She fears Nellie is pushing the doctor to fall in love with her. She's afraid Nellie is going to get hurt because she is too stubborn and selfish to listen to wisdom." Gran sighed. "It is always so much better to let the man do the chasing and catching," she repeated.

They worked on cookies until lunch time. The last pan came out of the oven just as Emily Stuart knocked on the kitchen door.

"We were wondering if Meg wanted to come sledding with us. It's cold, but it should be glorious out on the big hill." Emily hopped back and forth from one foot to the other, impatient for the answer.

Meg laughed. "I got up this morning hoping to do that very thing. It's warmer now so it won't be as miserable out there. Let me bundle up and get my boots. I'll be right out."

By the time she was ready, Gran had bagged cookies for the Stuart family and sent them over to their house. Emily was back along with several of her sisters, bundled to the eyes against the cold, giggling at the prospect of the adventure ahead.

Chapter Twenty

The big hill descended in front of them. Each year, the steep incline claimed victims, twisted ankles, scrapes and bruises, and sometimes even broken bones. A stand of trees along one side was the only way to successfully climb up the hill after the whirlwind ride down. Thankfully, you didn't have to climb the hill beforehand.

Meg stood with the girls looking down from the top of the hill. A few sledders were already there, taking turns skimming down. Many sledders could go down at the same time without fear of accidents, but if one didn't steer well, they would be in danger of the stand of trees that curved into the open area at the bottom on one side. Meg led the girls to the middle of the hill and organized them for the descent. Before long the first sled full of Stuarts was on its way down the hill.

Finally, the long awaited moment had come. Meg climbed on her sled and pushed off for the wild, exhilarating, breathtaking ride to the bottom. She whizzed at break neck speed, trees and other sledders flying past in a blur. The shrieks of terror and enjoyment tore from her of their own accord. At the bottom she slowed and tumbled off the sled, then moved out of the way of other sledders and started for the top again.

The ride was over so quickly, and the walk to the top so long, that each of them could only do it a few times before dark. But they did it with gusto, laughing, tumbling, flailing a the bottom, getting up covered in snow; cold, but having so much fun they didn't notice.

"One more time," Meg insisted, "and then we need to go home."

That last climb up the hill was the hardest. Without the anticipation of another trip down they noticed how tired their limbs were, how many bumps and bruises they had from their tumbles. They laughed and chattered all the way home. The youngest two girls were so tired they had to be pulled on the sleds.

"Come inside for something warm to drink!" insisted Emily.

Meg hadn't been to their house in a long time, but it was exactly how she remembered it. As an only child and living with her Gran, her life was calm and quiet. The Stuart house was bustling and busy. She listened to the girls' chatter as they told their parents about the afternoon. The youngest two girls acted it out. They all laughed at the stories and ate the treats their mother had set out as though they had never eaten before. The food was simple — brown bread and jam — but it was delicious after all their exercise.

"Does it seem loud compared to your quiet house?" Mrs. Stuart asked Meg as she offered a cup of hot chocolate.

Meg chuckled as she accepted the cup. "Yes, it does. I think I'd get overwhelmed if I was in it all the time. Well, I don't know. I worked in the children's ward in the hospital. It can get loud in there. I did alright." She grinned. "If I was living with it all the time, though, I might wish it would be quiet now and then."

Mrs. Stuart laughed, a merry, warm sound. "They come one at a time, so you don't get all the noise at once. It comes on so gradual that, one day they are all away, and you notice there isn't any chatter at all and you miss it."

Gran had supper waiting for Meg when she came in — heated leftovers with Gran's wonderful rolls. Meg couldn't believe how hungry she still was after her snack at the Stuart's. Now it was her turn, in the warmth of their little kitchen, to tell Gran all about sledding that afternoon. Then she told her about the short visit at the Stuart's house.

After supper, they iced the cookies and bagged them for Meg to take with her to the hospital in the morning. They cleaned the kitchen and put everything back in order.

"You should come with me tomorrow, Gran. Those children would love you." Meg insisted.

"I was thinking of seeing if Emily wanted to come and sew tomorrow after school. She was starting to catch on, but we stopped when I got sick. It gets so quiet here with you gone." Gran turned to the counter and finished wiping it.

"You could start again after Christmas, you know. We'll need to prepare for the bazaar. Folks will be looking for your preserves and fruitcakes. You could help Emily make something for it, too."

"I hadn't thought of that." Gran considered. "It would be fun. We could make so many things in a short time if we planned it right."

"So then you'll come with me tomorrow?" Meg asked eagerly.

"We'll see in the morning. I'm not promising. You'll get to introduce me to your young man next week anyway. Besides, someone has to stay here and look after things. It would be a long day for an old woman."

"You could sit the whole day and read books to the children," Meg said. "Well, I'm off to bed now, I think. My legs are so tired I don't know if I can climb those stairs. I might have to sleep down here in front of the fire."

She almost dragged herself up the steps to her room. Her bed was calling. Meg soon answered, falling into it and to sleep.

Chapter Twenty-one

The next day dawned warmer, but gray. Clouds threatened to dump more snow on them at any moment. Dr. Grey arrived at his normal time. Gran wasn't feeling well. Her rheumatism made it hard for her to move around and she was in a great deal of pain. Dr. Grey checked her over before they left and assured her all was well with her.

"We won't be able to stay all day, anyway. I suspect it will be snowing by noon. We'll need to be sure to get back before the roads get impassable. But don't worry about us, Mrs. Hollister. I'll bring Meg back safe and sound." He patted Gran's hand, then rose to leave.

Meg waited by the door with a large basket of the cookies they'd made the day before. She handed a bag to Dr. Grey, his name written on the outside. He grinned his thanks. They headed into the cold to the car.

The children were so happy to see Meg that morning. The room wasn't as full as it had been. The extra beds had been removed and not all of the remaining beds were occupied.

She led the children in singing Christmas carols and handed out the cookies. The room echoed with laughter and chatter. Then they got quiet and listened when Meg read the Christmas story. The morning passed more quickly than she'd imagined it would. Jack needed a visit before they left so, after a couple more carols, she excused herself, said goodbye, and wished them all a Merry Christmas.

Nurse Rogers met her in the hall as she walked to Jack's room. "After the holidays, it seems there won't be as much of a need for your help in the wards. Do you mind going back to doing the things you were doing before?"

Meg smiled. "I'd be happy to help however you need. The day by day work of rolling bandages or peeling potatoes will be a relief after the chaos of the last couple months."

"I agree," said Nurse Rogers. "Thank you. Everyone has grown accustomed to your help around here so you might find you get out a bit more than you did before."

Meg handed a bag of cookies to Nurse Rogers with a smile. There were quite a few left, more than she'd been expecting to have. "What should I do with these? It would be a shame to take them home with me. They were made for the people here."

"Why don't you hand them out ward by ward until they are gone? I'm sure no one will turn them down."

It took longer for Meg to reach Jack's bed that morning because she was spreading Christmas cheer to others in the hospital. She felt strange going to each bed and talking to these virtual strangers. They were all happy to see her. The little bags of cookies were gone before she reached Jack's bed, except for the one she'd saved for him.

"Merry Christmas!" she exclaimed as she had with all the other people she'd visited. "I brought a bag of Christmas cookies for you today. I hope you enjoy them! Where should I put them?"

"You can give them to me." Jack grinned at her. He perched on the edge of the bed. Meg handed him the bag of cookies. Jack opened it and looked inside. "I hope there are more of those wonderful sugar cookies. You made gingersnaps. I can smell them. My mom always makes those for Christmas, too. And snickerdoodles." He pulled one out and took a big bite. "MmmmMmm. Thank you so much, Miss. Your visit has brightened my day and improved my Christmas spirit."

Meg laughed at him. "I hope you have a wonderful Christmas, sir," she said as she backed toward the door.

"I intend to. There is this nice girl and her grandmother who've invited me to their house. I get to leave this boring hospital for a whole day. I can hardly wait. I think that girl must be an angel for inviting me like she did." He winked at Meg. "Her Gran is a good cook so the food ought to be amazing."

Meg dropped the play acting, and sank down on the bed next to Jack. "You can *not* believe what all Gran has planned for the meal. She's stuffing a turkey. We're having sweet potatoes, and regular potatoes, and green peas that we canned from the garden, and green beans from the garden, and pies, and a cake. Aunt Elaine is bringing some things, too. There might not be room for people at the dinner table."

Jack's grin expanded. "You have no idea how much I'm looking forward to it. They found crutches for me." He pointed at them leaning against the neighboring bed. "I've been practicing with them. I broke my leg when I was a kid so I've used them before. Here, watch."

He gripped the crutches and stood up, struggling for balance the whole time. Once he had them settled, one under each arm, he was able to shuffle up the center aisle with very little trouble. He came back and sank onto the bed. "Good thing your house isn't too large. It's tiring going even a short distance. I'll keep practicing. In a few days I should be pretty good at it."

"You are doing far better than I ever would if I tried," Meg said. "It looks like it's getting ready to snow. Dr. Grey wants to leave early. That's why I came by right now. I'd probably better head for the front door to see if he's ready. I'd hate to keep him waiting for me. He said to tell you he was coming for you Christmas morning. He didn't know what time he'd arrive. The nurses have agreed to take you to the front in a wheelchair so you don't have to walk all the way. It'll be here before you know it. I haven't been this excited for Christmas since I was a little kid."

Meg was home in time for lunch. After cleaning up from their meal, the afternoon stretched before her waiting to be filled. It felt good to sit and work on her handwork and think. They had decorated the house for Christmas the previous Saturday. The smell of the pine boughs filled the room. It always looked pretty at Gran's house for Christmas, but this year seemed better than it had in a while. Her mind wandered to everything that they still needed to do to get ready for the holiday. There would be a lot to accomplish, but she was eager to do all of it.

Chapter Twenty-two

Christmas morning dawned cold, but warmer than it had been for several days. A fresh dusting of snow had fallen in the night, turning the outdoors into a winter wonderland, and giving them a white Christmas. The pristine world outside glittered in the sunlight.

Gran and Meg discovered early morning Christmas treats along with the cinnamon rolls they'd made the night before, a little bag of candy sitting beside Meg's plate at breakfast, a tiny tin of tea for Gran from Meg. They exclaimed over the surprises, drank the coffee, and savored the rolls while still in their nightgowns and robes. They lingered over breakfast longer than normal, enjoying the quiet, bright morning.

Then both women got to work. They needed to finish their dinner preparations. Company would arrive in only a few hours. Meg wanted everything ready beforehand so she could enjoy the day. They had baked cookies and a pie in the days before. Gran was roasting a stuffed turkey. There would be cranberry sauce. Meg placed the sweet potatoes into the oven with the turkey, then ran to get dressed. Dr. Grey hadn't been specific about when he would arrive with Jack. She didn't want to get caught in her nightgown.

She didn't need to worry. They had enough time to finish the last minute touches on the food and set the table. They laid the table in the best china. Gran insisted on using a snow white table cloth and the Christmas napkins. Meg tucked final Christmas surprises for Jack into a stocking she had found.

They both heard the car turn onto their street at the same time. Meg whipped her apron off and hurried for the front door. "Do I look okay, Gran?" she asked. Her stomach fluttered with sudden nerves as her hands skimmed over her hair to tame any stray hairs that had escaped.

"Of course, dear. You look beautiful. Now, let's open the door for our guest." Gran's calm helped steady Meg.

Meg smoothed her dress, then made another pass over her hair and moved to answer the door.

A tall, sandy-haired young man climbed out of the car with Dr. Grey's help. Meg felt as though she was seeing Jack for the first time. She noticed his sparkling green eyes and square jaw. He was handsome. That fact had never been lost on her before, but this morning, out of the familiar surroundings of the hospital, she noticed it even more.

Jack made his way up the walk on his crutches. He managed despite the obvious effort it took. Dr. Grey closed the door of the car and waved to them all. "Merry Christmas!" he called, then got back in the car and drove away. Jack turned toward the departing car and waved, then continued his trip into the house.

"Come in! Come in!" Gran said, patting his arm, helping him over the ledge into the house.

"You must be Meg's Gran," said Jack, holding out his hand toward Gran.

"And you must be Meg's Jack." Gran ignored the outstretched hand and wrapped her arms around Jack for a hug. She squeezed him and slapped him hard on the back several times. Jack smiled over her shoulder at Meg.

Gran pulled away and Meg stepped forward to help Jack with his coat.

"Meg's Jack," Jack whispered as she helped him. "I like that."

Meg flushed. "I'm so glad you two can finally meet. You've heard enough about each other for me to feel you are already acquainted." Meg helped steady Jack. He shook one arm at a time out of his coat. Gran took the coat and hung it on a peg by the front door, next to her own and Meg's coats.

"Now, please come and sit for a while. Meg can get you something to drink and we can chat." Gran took charge and began to lead Jack into the front room.

"Gran, I was wondering if you had everything done for lunch," Jack asked, hesitating in the hallway.

"Well," Gran sounded uncertain, "I'm not sure. There are a few things we need to finish, but Meg can handle it."

"Why don't we all go to the kitchen. We can chat in there while you work," Jack suggested.

"I suppose that would be fine." Gran turned and led the way to the warm room, full of delightful smells and treats.

Jack wearily sank onto the chair Gran indicated, and set the crutches to the side. "It smells wonderful in here." He sighed in contentment, breathing in large lungfuls of the aromas. "I haven't smelled something this nice in a long, long time."

"Where is your family from?" asked Gran as she and Meg put the final touches on the food. Meg brought Jack a cup of coffee and set it on the table next to him with the cream and sugar.

"I'm from Indiana," he answered. "Dad has a big farm back there. Used to help him run it. Now my little brother helps out. Suppose I'll go back there after I'm done healing."

"Meg grew up in Ohio. That isn't far from Indiana." Gran commented.

"Really?" Jack said, giving Meg a puzzled look. "She's never mentioned that before. Come to think of it, aside from you and her aunt and cousin, she hasn't mentioned much about her family."

"It hasn't come up," Meg said without looking up from the potatoes she was mashing. "You've never mentioned anything about your parents or your brothers and sisters, either."

"Then I'm glad it did now." He smiled, settled back in his chair with his fingers interlocked behind his head. "My dad is working the farm his dad settled as a homestead. There's a big log house with a loft. The loft was us kids' room. The barn is sort of attached, but not completely. We get so much snow there in winter that one spring Dad got tired of it and built a walkway across.

"They have cows, sheep for the wool, pigs and chickens for the eggs. Mostly, though, he raises corn and wheat. Acres and acres of the stuff.

"I'm the oldest, and I have two younger brothers and a sister. One of my brothers was also off fighting in the war, though now it's over he'll be heading back home. My sister was a field nurse. The other brother stayed home to help Dad with the farm because he was too young to fight. I think he was planning on signing up if this thing kept going like it was, but now I think he wants to go off to college somewhere. He's waiting for me to get home and take over for him. Right now, I'm not sure how much good I'll be. A month ago I couldn't see how I'd ever walk again and here I am. Who knows where I'll be by spring. Now. Your turn."

Gran looked over at Meg. The two women were plating the food. Aunt Elaine and Nellie would be here any minute. Gran wanted things to sit on the table and "rest" as she called it. She nodded at Meg to encourage her to talk. Meg didn't know where to begin.

"Dad is…was Gran's son. He and my Mom lived in Ohio for a while before I was born. They weren't able to have children for a long time before they had me. Dad taught in a college out there. I'm an only child."

"Do you miss not having brothers and sisters?" he asked.

"Sometimes. But I have Nellie. She can be enough for two sisters. Speaking of which." They could hear a car coming down the road. It had to be Aunt Elaine.

Gran started toward the front door. Jack grabbed his crutches and, with colossal effort, pushed himself to his feet. Meg stayed to help him if he needed it, but he'd been practicing and accomplished the feat on his own. He grinned at her in triumph. He leaned toward her and whispered, "You'll have to tell me more later. I want to learn all I can about you."

Meg smiled at him. "I'm sure there will be time for us to talk after lunch."

Jack smiled back and shuffled up the hall on his crutches, while Meg turned to gather dishes to put on the dinner table.

Nellie breezed into the house with laughter and loud Christmas greetings. She shrugged out of her coat. Aunt Elaine carried in a basket with their food, which she took straight to the dining room table.

"Who do we have here?" Nellie exclaimed after hanging her coat and hat. She reached for Jack's hand and clutched it, shaking hands for a little too long. "I'm Nellie."

Meg cringed inwardly as she went back to the kitchen for more food. Gran was introducing Jack. Nellie asked him about his injuries. She gushed and exclaimed over his bravery in the face of such a trial. Meg turned away from all the noise. She hid herself in her kitchen work and rushed back and forth to the dining room to put the food on the table and have everything ready to eat.

After lunch and clean-up, Gran led the way to the front room. They all took seats around the room. Meg brought dining room chairs to make up the extra seats they needed. Then, they all grew quiet and listened as Gran read the Christmas story. Meg loved this tradition. Gran could quote the story, but she still got out her Bible every year and read it. Such feeling filled her voice. Sometimes she would break for little comments like "can you imagine how surprised they must have been when that angel appeared?" or "imagine having a baby in a barn!"

Then, they handed out gifts. Meg had knitted a scarf and mittens for Jack in her evenings at home. He was surprised speechless by them. Meg was so relieved they fit him, she almost didn't care if he liked them or not. Almost.

But he did. He put them on and admired them, showing them off to the group. "I don't have anything for you, Meg," he murmured for her ears alone. He was embarrassed. Meg sank onto the couch beside him. She started to assure him that, of course it was fine and she expected nothing from him when Nellie spoke out.

"Oh, she doesn't mind," Nellie said and giggled. She gave a dismissive way of her hand. "Meg is always so sweet about that kind of thing. She always remembers my birthday, but I forget hers almost every year. It doesn't bother her, though."

Meg flushed with embarrassment and stood to her feet once more. She turned away from Jack and faced Gran, sitting in her easy chair by the front window.

Gran opened Meg's gift for her — a pair of knit slippers and a shawl. "You're always cold in the morning, Gran, even in the summer. I thought you might like those while you waited for your morning coffee to warm you up."

"I'll enjoy them more often than that!" Gran exclaimed in delight and hugged the gifts to her chest.

There were gifts for them from Aunt Elaine and Nellie, and a little bag of chocolates that Uncle Daniel had sent for them to share with everyone for Christmas.

Meg slipped into the kitchen to put on another pot of coffee while everyone else settled in to talk and play card games and relax for the rest of the afternoon. She heard Aunt Elaine and Gran set up a game of bridge. Nellie decided to join them. She called for Jack to come and play the fourth player, but he declined. "Meg was telling me something earlier and didn't get to finish," Meg heard him say to the group. A moment later, his crutches sounded on the wood floor of the hall.

Meg was putting together a plate of cookies and other goodies to set out when Jack shuffled into the kitchen. She smiled at him as he entered the room and sank into the chair he'd used before.

"I see what you mean," he murmured so no one in the front room could hear. "She does delight in making sure she is the center of attention. I thought she already has a beau?"

Meg rolled her eyes, poured him a cup of coffee, then offered the plate of cookies. "To hear her talk, she does." She managed a sheepish smile. Then she took the plate of goodies into the front room. Leaving it with them, she returned to the kitchen and sat down across from Jack with her own cup of coffee and a cookie.

Jack munched his cookie. "Your Gran tells me you are the one who made all these. And all the goodies that have been making their way to my stomach the last few weeks."

Meg flushed and brushed imaginary crumbs from the table into her hand. "It doesn't matter as long as you enjoyed them."

"It matters to me," Jack said, his voice earnest and she looked at him. His eyes were just as intense. "You are a wonderful cook, Meg. I should be the one that is embarrassed because I assumed it was your Gran doing everything. I should have known otherwise. Now, I'd love it if you'd finish telling me about your family."

Meg didn't speak right away. She got up from the table to fetch a photograph hanging in the hall. Bringing it back she handed it to him as she sat down.

"Those are my parents and myself when I was a child." She pointed to the people in the picture as he looked at it.

"You look almost exactly like your Mom," he said.

"People say that all the time. Gran says I act like her, too."

"Where are they, now? Do they still live in Ohio? You mentioned a long time ago that you came to live with your Gran because she needed someone look after her."

Meg shook her head. She couldn't meet his eyes. It had been a long time since she talked about this to anyone. The pain was still fresh. If she tried to say too much she would cry. Meg fought back the tears so she could tell her story.

"Two years ago, a bad flu went through our college town in Ohio. My Dad got sick. Once it started going around the college it got pretty bad. He was among the first to fall ill. Mom stayed with him in the hospital. I was sick, too. They let us all be together. It was touch and go for me for a few days, but I got better. My Dad didn't. He died. About a week after he died, my Mom fell ill. She died, too. I think she gave up hope because he was gone. I was old enough that I could have stayed there and gotten a position at the mill in town. But Gran needed someone to live with her so I came here instead. I always loved coming here as a kid. The change was probably good for me. The memories here aren't filled with as much pain as they would have been in Ohio."

She stood, took the picture and rehung it on the wall. She needed a moment to regain control of her emotions. The last thing she wanted to do right now was cry in front of Jack Collins. She swallowed hard, past the huge lump in her throat and her burning eyes.

When she returned to the kitchen Jack was standing, but only using one crutch. She ducked her chin so he couldn't see her face, wouldn't notice her red-rimmed eyes. She tried to step around him, but he caught her around the waist with his free arm. Then he hugged her to himself. Meg gripped his shirt in tight fists. She could feel his ribs underneath. He was still so thin from the war and recovering from his injuries.

"I'm sorry," Jack whispered into her hair. "I didn't know. If I had known…" His voice faded and he pulled her closer to himself.

His compassion was her undoing. There, against his bony chest, with his arm firmly holding her, the tears came. Meg cried into his shoulder. The pain, the ache of her parents' death and and the loss and loneliness she felt on holidays, was so hard, but with his arm tight around her, she felt like he understood and that feeling brought comfort she hadn't anticipated. Her sobs ebbed. She released his shirt and smoothed the fabric. Her tears had wet his shirt.

Meg stepped away from Jack. He slowly, reluctantly released her. She looked up at him.

"I'm sorry for getting your shirt wet." Meg wiped at his shirt with her handkerchief, then used it to dab the remaining tears from her eyes.

Jack's hand still stroked her arm. "It was a pleasure to get to be the shoulder *you* cry on for a change." He smiled, his face so close to her own.

Meg returned his smile and stepped away. She took a deep breath and sat down in her chair before she continued speaking. "I hadn't been back in a hospital until this fall, when we went to volunteer. I had a difficult time at first. I was glad we didn't have anything to do with people for a while. Then, of course, I met you and my view of hospitals changed."

A sudden knock sounded on the kitchen door. Meg startled at the abrupt sound, then hurried to answer it. Emily Stuart stood on the back steps with a plate of goodies.

"Mom wanted these brought over last night, but I went to get my boots and set them down on the table in my room and forgot until morning! Please don't tell her that I didn't bring them until today!" she pleaded.

Meg couldn't stifle the giggle. Emily could be so absent-minded. Emily giggled with her. Then Emily pulled a smaller package out of her pocket.

"I almost forgot this, too! It's for your Gran to say thanks for trying to teach me how to sew. I'll have to go right in there and give it to her. Oh! This must be Jack. Mrs. Hollister told me about you during our sewing lessons. I'm Emily. Emily Stuart. I live next door and, well, Merry Christmas!" She breezed out of the kitchen and down to the front room.

"Well! She's.... spunky," Jack stuttered, at a loss for words.

"She has four younger sisters. She has to be," Meg said. The plate contained fudge and other chocolate treats. She passed the plate to Jack, then took a piece herself. "Mrs. Stuart makes the best fudge I've ever tasted. Maybe we should keep this in here and not share it with anyone in the living room."

Emily came breezing back through. "Look at these wonderful gloves! Your Gran is amazing! Five fingers for each hand and they all fit! Mine would be lopsided and one side bigger than the other. These would have been so nice last week when we went sledding, wouldn't they? Now it will have to snow again so I can use them when we sled. I can hardly wait to show the girls. See you sometime!" And she was gone as suddenly as she had appeared.

Jack stared at Emily's departing back. "Does she breathe when she talks? You went sledding last week? You like sledding?"

"Of course! What normal person doesn't like sledding?"

"Well, my sister for one. Mom would make her go for the exercise. I didn't know girls went voluntarily. Where do you sled around here?"

"There is a huge hill at the town park. Every time we get a decent snow most of the town's children turn out to take a few trips down," Meg said. "It is a *long,* tiring walk back up. But the trip down is worth every step of the climb."

"You have to show me sometime," Jack begged. "I love hills like that. It's too bad I can barely walk or we could go over there right now and take a look, maybe even try it!"

"Young man, you must let yourself heal and try not to injure yourself again, do you understand me?" Meg frowned, shaking her finger at him. "One thing at a time. Walking before running, sledding, or climbing!"

"Yes, ma'am. I promise to behave myself and not try anything foolish. Yet." He gave Meg one of his rare grins and winked at her.

The afternoon waned. Aunt Elaine had offered to return Jack to the hospital. They would need to leave soon in order to be back before it was completely dark. The group gathered in the front room and sang Christmas carols together until it was time to go. Then Meg packed some leftovers for Jack to eat for supper when he got back. She packed another bag of cookies and other treats for him as well.

Nellie was in the front room chattering to Jack. Meg could see his polite smile in her mind's eye. She had to admit it pleased her that he wasn't the least bit interested in Nellie.

∞

Jack settled against the seat in the back of Aunt Elaine's car. The long day had worn him out and he struggled to focus on what Nellie was saying. She prattled on and on, content to keep talking as long as he gave a grunt now and then that implied he'd heard what she said. She was telling some story about Meg when they were children. In

110

fact, she'd been telling one story after another about Meg for the whole drive.

He sighed and leaned his head against the window behind him. The rattle and bounce of the car jarred his head against the glass but at least his eyes were closed.

"Nellie," said Aunt Elaine, "we appear to have worn Mr. Collins out today. Why don't you give him a chance to rest while we drive?"

Jack risked a peek at Nellie after her mother spoke. It baffled him how a girl Nellie's age would need to be rebuked by her mother in such a way. His own sister would have been embarrassed. Nellie pouted at her mother, but turned to face the front window and fell silent. *She's used to getting her own way with everything,* thought Jack as he dropped his eyelids shut once more. Then he sighed and straightened in his seat.

"I'm fine, Mrs. Reynolds. I'm not used to this much activity in a day and I've tired myself out. But I'll be fine until we get back to the hospital."

"As long as you're sure about that." Aunt Elaine looked at him in the mirror.

"I'm sure."

Nellie's coy smile had reappeared and she picked up with the story she'd been telling as though she'd never stopped. Jack fixed a polite smile on his own mouth and made sure he grunted in all the right places.

Jack was ready to exit the car the minute Aunt Elaine pulled up to the curb. An orderly appeared with a wheelchair. Jack's legs were stiff after the drive and, even though he'd started before they arrived, it took him a minute to work his way out of the car. By the time he was ready to get out, Nellie had come around to help. She grabbed his arm and tried to haul him up by it. The skin in his legs felt like it was on fire, wrenching, tearing. Jack stifled a groan and shrugged out of her grip. She was forcing him to move too fast.

"I think I'd prefer if the orderly helped me," he managed through clenched teeth.

111

The orderly had been waiting for his opening. He stepped up to the car, gripped Jack under the arms, and with one smooth motion, lifted him up and swung him into the waiting chair. Jack hadn't needed to straighten his legs after all.

Jack heaved a sigh of relief that the ordeal was over. Then he smiled up at Aunt Elaine. "Thanks for the ride back. I've had a wonderful day."

"I'm happy to help. But you have Meg to thank for the day. The whole thing was her idea. You rest well and get better." She finished with a wave as she stepped back into the car and put it in gear.

Nellie stood to the side, scowling at the lot of them. "It wasn't all Meg's idea. I helped her plan it."

Jack plastered a smile on his face. "Yes. Well, thank you, too." The orderly turned the chair and pushed him toward the hospital, leaving Nellie staring after him. A look of uncertainty flickered across her face. She tried to smile at him but it morphed into a frown. Jack flicked his hand in a wave as they entered the hospital doors. He heard a car door close and the car motored away.

Jack lay in bed that night listening to the men around him breathe. Some still moaned in pain in their sleep. He thought over the day and how wonderful it had been. He wished he'd thought to find a way to get a gift for Meg. He should have known she'd make something for him.

Jack's mind wandered over the events of the last year. He'd been in an army training camp last Christmas. His parents had sent him a box filled with goodies. No such box had arrived this year. Jack suspected that was because he hadn't communicated with them since he'd arrived at the hospital. Shame filled him. He had a family that loved him back home, but he'd distanced himself from them in every way he could.

He thought about France. For the first time, he wasn't filled with horror at the thought. He wondered how the other men in his unit were doing. Were they on their way home? Had some of them arrived in time for Christmas with their families?

Cavanaugh. Jack hadn't thought about the man in weeks. He'd shoved all memory of him to the back of his mind and hadn't let it out. He still owed Cavanaugh's widow and baby a letter.

With a grunt, Jack pushed himself up and sat on the edge of the bed. He forced his legs to relax and bend. Then he felt around inside the drawer next to his bed for matches and lit the lantern next to the bed. Light flooded the little drawer. Jack turned the lantern down. No need to draw unnecessary attention. He found the photo Cavanaugh had handed him. It still had the man's dried blood on it. Jack cringed as the memories of that night flooded his mind. He pulled a sheet of paper and a pencil from the drawer and closed it. Then he set about writing a letter he'd been avoiding all these months.

Once the words started they flowed and Jack couldn't stop. He told Cavanaugh's wife of the fun times they'd had in training, of the rain and mud in France and Cavanaugh's indomitable spirit. Through barely muffled sobs, he told her Cavanaugh's last words, his declaration of his undying love.

I hope one day to find a woman I can love like this, he wrote, *so fully, so completely, to my dying breath.*

A sudden realization seized him and he dropped the pencil onto the paper. "I think I *have* found a woman like that."

He left the paper on the table and blew out the lantern. With effort, he swung his legs onto his bed. It didn't hurt as bad to put them back up as it had to drop them down. Maybe the motion was easier. Or maybe his mind was fixed on something, or someone, else — a girl with brown hair and brown eyes that had taken such good care of him the last few weeks.

Jack fell asleep remembering the wonder of holding her in his arms earlier in the day. He hoped, no, planned, to make sure that wasn't the last time he got to do it.

Chapter Twenty-three

Meg felt listless in the week after Christmas. Planning and preparing for the holiday had taken up so much of their time. Now she felt like she had nothing to do with herself. The Ladies Aid Bazaar was coming up at the end of January. They needed to prepare for it. Meg was thankful they'd planned ahead and made apple butter to sell at the bazaar, but she didn't know what else they were going to make.

Gran had some ideas. She suggested Meg knit a blanket. She was going to piece a quilt. As soon as Christmas was over, Gran brought the scrap boxes out and they started work on their projects. Meg helped cut the quilt pieces during the week she was at home between the holidays. She helped by ironing seams after Gran sewed them. She made a good start on her knitted blanket. The scrap box held many rolls of yarn in bright colors for her to use.

Meg enjoyed seeing the projects take shape under their fingers. She usually made small items like the mittens for Jack. She enjoyed the challenge of the blanket she was knitting.

A heavy snow fell that week and Meg made another trek to the Big Hill with the Stuart girls. This time Dr. Coburg and Nellie came with them. Nellie, of course, refused to make the trip down the hill even once. She said it was unladylike, with a significant look in Meg's direction. Meg just laughed, got back on her sled and hurtled down the hill with the youngest Stuart girl on board with her. By the time they'd dragged the sled back up the hill, Nellie was sitting primly on a log inside the tree line sporting a haughty expression. She refused to meet Meg's eye.

Meg watched each of her charges as they flung their bodies and sleds down the hill at breakneck speed. The sun had sunk low in the afternoon sky when Emily and Penny Stuart decided to take one final trip down the hill. Half-way down, the rope they used to steer the sled broke. With shrieks of terror and flailing limbs, they tried to slow down and stay straight on their course. They were successful until they reached the bottom and their sled veered toward the trees. Emily managed to tumble off in time, but Penny plowed, along with the sled, right into a tree. She sprawled unconscious on the ground.

Meg cried out in terror, threw herself on her sled, and raced down the hill. The trip down felt like an eternity, though she reached the bottom after only a few seconds.

Penny was pale and hadn't moved. Meg touched her hands and feet. They twitched. She patted the girl's face. Her eyes fluttered, then opened. "My head..." she murmured, then her eyes slid shut again and she winced in pain.

"Can you move your arms or your legs?" Meg demanded, panicked.

"I think so." Penny answered, moving both. "Did I break the sled?"

"Don't worry about the sled, sweetheart. If it's broken it can be fixed. Let's worry about you for a little while." Meg felt the girls head and shoulders and gently pressed on her collar bone. A small groan escaped Penny's mouth.

Dr. Coburg arrived at the bottom and took over the examination. After a few minutes he decided they could move her. They loaded her onto Meg's sled and began dragging it up the hill. The steep hill made a smooth trip impossible. Penny moaned every time the sled jerked. Dr. Coburg managed most of the trip, but near the top, Emily and Meg took over.

Nellie waited for them wringing her hands, incapacitated by a fit of hysterical sobbing. "Is she okay? Is she okay? Oh, the poor baby! What happened?"

Dr. Coburg took Nellie by the shoulders and gave her a tiny shake. "You have to get yourself under control," he commanded her.

"She will be fine, none of her injuries are life threatening. We need to get her home so I can better assess them."

"Oh, of course!" Nellie sucked in a few shaky breathes and turned to hurry down the road ahead of them.

"Nellie." Dr. Coburg sounded annoyed now. "You need go home. I won't be able to accompany you, but I'm sure you'll be fine. It's still long before dark. The less confusion we bring to this already muddled situation the better."

Meg moved ahead of Dr. Coburg and Nellie with the rest of the girls. She and Emily towed Penny on the sled. The lovers needed to have their spat and be done with it. In private. Nellie had always been dramatic, but hysterics was a little much, even for her. She'd frightened two of the younger girls and they were crying hard, convinced the situation was far worse than it was.

"Hush, little ones, hush!" Meg crooned. She dropped the sled rope and hugged the sobbing girls to herself. Even Emily looked scared. Meg could see she needed to calm them all. "Penny is going to be fine, aren't you, Penny?"

The girl managed a weak smile and nodded. "My head hurts really bad. And my shoulder."

"Dr. Coburg will check you when we get to your house. He is a very good doctor. He helped my Gran get better earlier this fall when she was sick. Remember?" They all nodded. "You scared us all, Penny. But I think, in the end, things aren't so bad as they seemed a little while ago."

Meg's quiet words calmed them. Emily took the little girls' hands. Meg picked up the sled rope. They trudged toward home trying not to jolt or jar the injured girl on the sled. The little girls looked less frightened, though they clung to Emily as if their life depended on it. They cut glances at Meg and Penny. If Meg said things were going to be okay, then they probably would be okay.

"We'll help Penny into your house and the rest of you can come to my house for something warm to drink and some cookies. We still have Christmas cookies we need to eat up before they turn into rocks." Meg infused as much cheery confidence into her voice as she could. Their faces brightened. Cookies made everything better.

Dr. Coburg caught up with them as they turned onto the street toward home. Nellie wasn't with him. Meg had been able to hear the heated tones of their conversation carried by the thin, cold winter air. He looked strained. He forced himself to smile at Meg, then checked Penny. Taking the sled's rope from Meg, he pulled it the rest of the way to their house.

Mr. and Mrs. Stuart observed their strange approach and met them at the door. Mr. Stuart lifted his little girl and carried her into the house, followed by his wife and the doctor. Meg ushered the other girls over to the kitchen door at Gran's house.

They pounded and shuffled their way out of wet hats, gloves, coats, and boots, and into the warm kitchen where Gran was stirring soup. Meg reached for the cookie jar and the teapot. Settling young bodies in a small space was interesting but, with Emily's help, they managed to get it done. The girls filled the room with noise and warmth and laughter. Meg made cocoa and passed mugs of it around. They finished the rest of the cookies along with a small section of cake that was left.

The whole tale of the sledding party and accident was recounted and dramatically represented in glorious detail to a captive Gran. She asked questions in the appropriate places and made light of the events so little girls wouldn't think they should worry.

Dr. Coburg knocked on the kitchen door as Gran was reaching for bowls in which to serve the soup to the hungry bellies seated at her table. He told them they could go home if they liked, but to please let Penny rest for at least the next couple of days.

They fought their way back into wet hats, coats, boots, and gloves with more chattering and giggling, then the whole gaggle made their way home.

"Whew!" Gran exclaimed when Meg shut the door and the noise faded into the night. "It felt like there were ten girls in here and not just four!"

Meg laughed out loud. It was so true! How on earth did Mrs. Stuart keep calm all the time? She turned to Dr. Coburg.

"How is Penny?" she asked as she placed bowls and spoons on the table. "Would you like to eat supper with us? It will save you having to cook when you get home. Unless, of course, you already have plans."

"Yes, thank you," he answered. "It would be a help to eat with you. I don't have any plans at all and the soup smells wonderful. I guess all that sledding gives one an appetite."

Meg reached for another place setting as the doctor continued talking.

"She will be fine. You probably noticed that she'd broken her collar bone. There's a possibility of a fracture on that same arm, but I put the whole thing in a sling and gave strict orders for her to not use it for several weeks. She has a concussion as well. I'm quite sure that, at least at first, keeping her from moving won't be a problem."

Meg was nervous that the conversation around the table would be awkward, but Gran kept it moving. She asked questions and told stories to entertain their guest.

Finally she asked. "I heard you are moving to Walton sometime soon. I hope we don't stop seeing you around here!"

"News gets around," he answered and smiled at Gran. "Yes, the practice here is slow so I'm going to start working at the hospital there. They need my help. It's easier for me to move than it is for Dr. Grey. Besides, if he needs help here I'll still be close enough to assist him until your son-in-law comes back."

"I guess you'll be seeing our girls, then," Gran said. "They go back on Monday to start volunteering again."

"Oh, really?" Dr. Coburg turned to Meg. "I hadn't heard that you were going back. I'm glad to hear it."

"We still won't see much of you. They need us back at more menial and less obvious work for a while," Meg said.

"They're getting more soldiers in January sometime so you might be surprised what you end up doing. That's part of the reason

I'm moving there. The need is great and they can't keep enough staff for the patients. I'm looking forward to it. Small town life is less eventful than I'm used to. The quiet was nice for a while, but I find I miss the activity of the city."

Meg thought back to their conversation when Gran had been sick. She wasn't surprised at all he was changing what he thought about their small town. Once a city boy, always a city boy. She supposed it applied to girls, too. She wasn't going to blame him. If she suddenly had to move from this quiet little town to Walton, she would be miserable. She'd grown up in a town the size of Hollis.

They finished eating. The doctor left for home, leaving the two ladies enjoying the quiet. They cleared the table and washed the dishes in silence. It wasn't until they were in the front room each working on their projects that either of them spoke.

"Did you notice that he never once mentioned Nellie?" asked Gran.

"I did find that curious," Meg said. "But maybe he isn't in a position for it to be as serious as she would like."

"That could be. But my instinct on it is that he isn't any more interested in a little country girl than he is in a little country town."

"Gran, that isn't fair!" Meg was shocked at her Gran's words. "Besides, Nellie acts like a city girl."

"I guess time will tell," Gran said and turned back to her work. "But I think you'll find I'm right. This isn't the first time I've seen this happen."

Chapter Twenty-four

The first day back to the hospital went just as Meg expected it would. They settled in to work in the familiar little sewing room.

Nellie heaved a dramatic sigh and settled in front of the sewing machine. "I guess I'll sew first."

Meg moved to pick up the first old sheet to tear into strips. The stack was no where near as high as it had been. The mending pile next to Nellie stretched above their heads. Nellie picked an apron from the top of the pile and bent to reattach a pocket.

"All the excitement happened when I was sick," Nellie said. She sighed again. "I wish I hadn't missed all that."

Meg squeezed her shoulder and both girls returned to their work.

"I want a new dress."

Meg blinked, startled at the change in subject.

Nellie continued before Meg had a chance to respond. "I asked Mom, but she said all my clothing was fine. She said it's a frivolous expense. If Dad was here, he'd have already gotten me one. He's the town doctor. We have to keep up appearances."

Meg had never considered this before. She opened her mouth to say something but Nellie went on.

"I'm so sick of everything in my closet. I've been wearing most of it for a couple years now. Look how shabby this dress has gotten." She dropped the apron into a pile on its own and waved her hand at the dress she was wearing. Then she grabbed another piece of mending. "It makes me physically ill to look at them. Mom doesn't care. She thinks I need to get more use out of them."

Meg stole a glance at her own dress. She hadn't had anything new in a couple years, either. When her parents had died, Gran had helped her remake some of her mom's dresses to fit Meg. Meg loved them. When the pain of losing her parents had been at its worst, she felt wrapped in her mom's arms every time she wore them. Then, with the war going on in Europe, a new dress had seemed like a luxury she could easily forgo.

Nellie had continued speaking and her voice cut through Meg's reverie.

"I wish Philip wasn't moving to Walton. I'm going to miss him so! He's been looking for a place when he works his shifts here. That's why he hasn't been around town much. He found a place right before Christmas and will be moving this next week. I think he's got plenty of work in Hollis, but Mom says he needs steadier income than he was getting in our little village. She thinks he wants to get married and he can't get married on the salary of a village doctor."

She paused for breath and to pick up another piece of mending. "Do you think he really wants to get married? What if he's saving so he can ask me once Dad comes back from Boston?" Nellie clasped her hands in front of her and turned shining eyes to Meg.

Meg opened her mouth to respond, but Nellie had turned back to her work and was talking.

"If that's the case, I'm so glad we got our first fight out of the way. He walked me home from church on Sunday." She turned coy eyes to Meg. "He even offered me his arm in town where everyone could see it." She looked back at her work. "He said he was wrong for sending me away and that maybe I could have helped the little girl get home. I'm good with children, you know."

Meg rolled her eyes. Nellie barely tolerated children.

"He said he wants children. Several of them. Two or three at least. I don't know if I want that many, but I'm willing to try for his sake. Besides, with him being a doctor and all the responsibilities that would come from being his wife, I'd *have* to get a nanny when they are little and a governess when they get older." She tossed her hair and dropped the mended item on the finished pile.

Meg finished the sheet she'd been tearing and carefully folded all the items in the mended pile.

Nellie continued talking, taking no notice of Meg. *She must be lonely,* Meg thought. *She needs someone to listen to her, just like I do. I have Gran. She doesn't have...* Meg hesitated. Nellie had Aunt Elaine. Meg gritted her teeth and pulled harder than necessary on the sheets she was ripping. Nellies prattle grated on her more and more as the hours passed. The subject always came back around to the same thing: Dr. Philip Coburg.

Meg had never been more relieved when the lunch hour arrived. The girls took their sack lunches and made their way to the dining room. Meg hadn't had time to eat there for the last several months, though sometimes she'd seen Phoebe or Sarah in passing and waved. Now both girls were sitting at a table in the middle of the room. They motioned for Meg and Nellie to join them.

"Are you excited for the bazaar?" Phoebe asked as soon as the girls were seated.

"I can hardly wait. We started preparing for it last fall," Meg said.

"Did your Gran make her apple butter? I love her apple butter!" Sarah gushed while she clutched her chest and closed her eyes in a fit of ecstasy.

Meg laughed at her dramatics. "We made apple butter, and preserves, and jelly, and pie filling, and sauce, and anything else we could think to make with apples. Gran's trees gave us a bumper crop this fall."

"Good. You can count on me to buy some of the butter at least. What else are you making?"

Meg hesitated. She didn't want to say anything about the quilt or blanket, just in case they weren't finished in time.

Phoebe gripped Meg's arm. "Did you girls hear the news?"

"Oh! You have to hear this!" Sarah said. "We should have told them right away."

Phoebe allowed a dramatic pause and all three of the other girls leaned forward in anticipation. "The Ladies Aid has organized a ball after the auction. A real ball. With an orchestra and old fashioned waltzes and everything."

Nellie gasped and turned to Meg whose eyes had widened with excitement.

"I've never been to a ball before. Have you?"

Meg shook her head. How she wanted to go! But she doubted she'd be able to. How would Gran get home? What would she wear? She had nothing suitable. She thought back to Nellie's monologue in the sewing room and had to stifle a laugh. She'd been so content with her clothing then. Now all she could think about was how to put together a dress fit for a ball from her meager clothing.

Meg shifted her focus to the conversation that had moved on without her.

"I'll figure out something to wear. Mom has to let me get a new dress for the ball," Nellie said.

"I have more news," said Sarah to Phoebe. "Not as exciting as the ball, but helpful all the same."

"What is this news?" Phoebe rested her elbows on the table on either side of her empty lunch bag and rested her chin on her folded hands.

"Some of the rich women in town got together and bought fabric to use for the bazaar. They said with the war just finished, many people would have used up their fabric and wouldn't have been able to buy more. One of the ladies is keeping it at her house and you can come over and choose whatever you want, as long as you use it for the bazaar."

"I'd like to see it if I could," said Meg.

"Sure," said Sarah. "I can take you to her house this afternoon."

"Maybe we can go when my aunt comes to pick us up." Meg looked at Nellie for confirmation and received a shrug in reply. Nellie had no interest in the fabric unless she could use it to make a dress for herself.

"I'll meet you in the lobby later this afternoon, then," said Sarah and Meg agreed.

Meg was excited as they headed back to work in the sewing room. Gran had been talking about how she'd always made aprons, frilly pillow cases, and little napkin sets in the past, but this year she didn't have the fabric to do it. The quilt top was finished. Gran was quilting it.

The Stuarts also had a sewing machine and Meg knew they'd put fabric to good use if she brought it to them. If they worked together, they could have many beautiful things to sell.

The afternoon was much more pleasant than the morning. They chatted about the bazaar and the ball. Both girls tried to figure out if they had something they could wear for it. Unlike the morning, the afternoon flew by. Meg looked at the clock and could hardly believe that it was time to stop working and go visit her soldier. Since Christmas, she'd been thinking of him as that — "her soldier" — despite all her protestations to Gran.

"I want to check on some of the people who'd been sick before Christmas, see how they are doing. Tell your mom to wait, if she arrives before I do," Meg told Nellie and made her escape. If Nellie came to visit Jack, the visit wouldn't be the same.

Jack was sitting in a chair at the end of his bed when she arrived. He looked worn out. He'd propped a cane against the chair beside him. He grinned when she came in.

"I have news!" he exclaimed.

"You too? It seems like everyone has news today. I'm away for two weeks and the whole place gets news!" Meg leaned against the metal footboard on Jack's bed.

"I've been working hard for the last few weeks. I've gotten where I can bear weight better on my ankles. The doctor said more soldiers were coming in on the next boat, so he's wanting those of us who can manage on our own to be discharged from the hospital and find a place to live nearby. He doesn't want me heading back to Indiana yet. He said I have to stay close so they can be sure that infection doesn't set in. I've been working this afternoon to walk without those crutches. I think I can do it. I'll need a job and a place to live, of course, once the doctor clears me to live on my own. What do you think of that?" he exclaimed.

"That is exciting!" Meg grinned at him. Then her smile faltered. "But it will mean I can't visit when I'm at the hospital. When do you get to leave?"

"Don't you worry. I won't be going far. I'll still be able to see you." Jack reached out and ran the back of his fingers down her jaw. "The doctor wasn't sure when I could leave, but probably in the next week or two." He shifted in his chair and leaned forward. "Your turn. What news did you hear today?"

"The Ladies Aid bazaar is coming up at the end of this month. Every year they hold a sale and an auction, but this year they're also holding a ball. The news is, they are getting a small orchestra to play for it. Gran might not let me come, but I'm going to ask her anyway." Meg was excited despite her uncertainty. She hesitated. "Now that I think about it, your news is better than mine."

Jack chuckled. "It's still pretty exciting. I guess. My Mom and sister were always the ones to be involved in those kinds of events. I wasn't all that interested in dancing so I guess I probably wouldn't have gone except they made me. That was a long time ago. I've seen the posters for the bazaar hanging around the hospital. Are you making anything?"

"I'm making a knitted blanket and Gran is making a quilt. They'll both go in the silent auction. We also made apple butter, among other things, last fall. It's quite popular at the bazaar. One of the nurses told me about some fabric that was donated. I'm going to look at it when Aunt Elaine comes to see if we can use any of it."

"So, what have you been doing since Christmas?" Jack asked, changing the subject. He leaned his head back against the wall behind him and waited for Meg to talk.

Meg told him about the excitement of Penny's sledding accident. She told him about working to get the quilt top finished before she started back at the hospital again. She told him about Dr. Coburg's strange visit over dinner and how he was planning to move to Walton.

"Interesting," Jack said. "Seems country life doesn't agree with him after all."

"Gran said almost the same thing," said Meg, surprised by his comment.

"Your Gran is a smart woman. She notices things. I'm sure she's pegged this Doctor pretty close. I can only comment from a man's perspective, but he's not acting like he's in love with anyone from your village."

"Nellie says that he is trying to get steady income so they can start courting," Meg said.

Jack snorted a laugh. "I doubt it! He'd find a way if it was possible and he really wanted it. No, you watch, after he's been living in town for a week or so while he'll become an item with a girl here, probably a nurse."

"I doubt he'll be so predictable." Meg rolled her eyes. "He's too nice of a person to do that to Nellie."

"Meg, has it occurred to you that he might not have figured it out that Nellie is interested in him? And if he has, in his mind he's done nothing to encourage a relationship. He might be trying to get away from Hollis to be free of any inference she might be making. It's as simple as that."

Meg sighed. "Nellie is going to be broken hearted. Not that I'd ever be able to warn her. She talks about him all the time. She wouldn't believe a word I said if I tried to tell her the feeling isn't mutual. She'd think I was jealous, and trying to be mean and vengeful. This is probably a lesson she'll have to learn the hard way."

A thought occurred to her. "Dr. Coburg isn't going to be living in the apartment behind the grocery any more. The rent would be cheap. Chances are good that Mr. Miller would give you a job stocking shelves. He and his children do it, but it's hard for him to keep up when they're in school. I could look into it for you, if you want. I don't know what jobs are like here in Walton. Or places for rent, for that matter."

Jack considered it. "I'd have to check with the doctor to see if they'd let me live so far away. However, I would be close to Dr. Grey. He's been in to check me several times. I'll think about it. The thought of having to look for a job is daunting especially since walking is still so difficult. Everything there is closer together. The army liaison didn't sound hopeful that I'd find a job in Walton."

Meg glanced at the clock and jumped to her feet. "I have to go."

"Why all the rush to get away?" he teased.

"I have to go meet the girls so we can pick some fabric."

Jack stood to his feet and, taking his cane, walked to the door. "I'll walk you to the end of the hall. I need the practice." He offered his arm. Meg slipped her hand into the crook of his elbow. He escorted her down the hall. When they reached the corner, he leaned closer. "I'll see you in a couple days." He whispered and caught her hand when she released his arm. He squeezed her fingers. His face was so close to her own. Those dear, beautiful green eyes scanned her face. Meg's breath hitched. She tore her gaze from his. The spell broken, she pulled away, smiled up at him, turned, and hurried to the lobby.

Chapter Twenty-five

The fabric was beautiful. They picked all they wanted. For Meg, it felt like Christmas all over again. She chose far more fabric than she thought they could work up between now and the bazaar. The lady said to bring back what they didn't use or save it for next year.

Meg had to offer an explanation for the pile of cloth she carried in the door. Gran admired each piece, the patterns, the way it felt.

Mrs. Stuart was just as impressed with the fabric when she came over to see it. Excitement sparkled in her eyes as she looked through it. "I can work while the girls are at school. Maybe even get their help in the evenings. It would be good for them," she said.

"Why don't you bring your machine over here during the day and we can work together?" Gran said.

"I'd enjoy that," said Mrs. Stuart. They made plans to sew together the next morning, then Mrs. Stuart returned home.

That evening as they ate their supper, Meg told Gran about Jack's upcoming release from the hospital. He needed a place to stay and a job. Gran agreed she should inquire with Mr. Miller about the apartment Dr. Coburg was vacating, and a possible job.

Meg's mind flitted from one event of the day to another as she lay in bed that night. Try as she might to stop them, her thoughts kept returning to the massive amount of sewing ahead and the possibility of Jack moving to Hollis. She stayed awake long into the night before falling into a fitful sleep.

Meg woke to sunlight streaming through the window. She fought to open still-tired eyes and lay there for a few minutes, enjoying the warmth of her blankets. Then she pushed back the covers, got up and dressed.

Meg could tell Gran was having trouble getting herself moving this morning, too. Her arthritis was bothering her. She didn't complain as she made the coffee but she winced with every movement. When Meg handed her a full cup of coffee, she wrapped her knobby fingers around it and sighed with relief.

"This cold doesn't help my arthritis at all," she said.

Mrs. Stuart came over mid morning, little Penny in tow. The other girls were at school. Penny settled herself on the couch, moaning with every movement.

"I know how she feels," Gran said, rubbing her knuckles. "I'm aching pretty badly today."

"I don't know which she complains of more, her head or her collar bone." Mrs. Stuart shook her head. "I'm having all I can do to keep her busy, but not up. Maybe our work will entertain her enough so she won't feel the need to mope."

"Let me get her some picture books to look at." Meg suggested. "She needs something new to keep her busy for a while." She grabbed Gran's shawl and draped it over the old lady's shoulders. "In the meantime, this should help your aches and pains."

Before they could begin, they had to decide what they were making and which fabric they would use for it. Each of the women inspected the cloth. Then they divided it into stacks to use for aprons, or table cloths and napkins, or throw pillows. Scraps could be used for pot holders or handbags. Mrs. Stuart planned to get Emily's help with the sewing after school every day.

Once they were organized they all worked on cutting the fabric into the pieces they would sew. They visited as they worked. The day flew by in a blur of activity. The pile of things they'd cut out to be sewn would keep them busy for several days at least.

The work at the hospital the next day seemed easy compared to the cutting and sewing Meg had done the day before. After lunch, Nurse Rogers brought Nellie and Meg to the children's ward to entertain the children. It was a slow day, but the soldiers were arriving at the end of the week and she needed all the nurses preparing for that.

Meg told stories. Then they chose a familiar nursery tale. She and some of the children who weren't as sick, told it to the rest, each one saying the lines of one of the characters. They sang songs in a round and she read to them. Now and then she took breaks to check on the very sick ones, she soothed the feverish, and adjusted bedding so the ones who were quite sick could sit up and see what the rest were doing. She tried to keep the noise down so if anyone wanted to rest they could. Meanwhile, Nellie sat in a corner, afraid to come out and do anything with the children. After a while, she disappeared.

Meg was exhausted when the ward nurse returned. She had a minute to run up to Jack's room before it was time to leave. She saw Nellie talking to Dr. Coburg in a hall.

Jack was sitting in the chair while a lady cleaned around his bed. She was wiping walls and had stripped the sheets. A broom stood at the ready for her to tackle the floor.

"Let's go for a walk!" Jack suggested and struggled to his feet. Standing required a lot of effort and still took a while for him to accomplish. Often, the scar tissue tore open and bled without Jack noticing. Today was no exception. But he led her out of the room and into the hall.

"I've been offering and offering to help her clean, but she won't let me. Keeps calling me 'you poor boy' and then gets back to work. I'm so glad to see you. I need something to distract me." They walked slowly up one side of the hall, then turned and made their way back. Jack's steps were halting, but steady. He'd improved since she saw him last.

"They want me out of here on Friday since I can live on my own. I've been thinking about what you said. If that place at the grocery is available, I'd really appreciate it. It would be a great place to start. If I can't work for the grocer, maybe I can get a job with someone else in town. I'd rather live there than here any day. I should have told you to check on Monday."

"I'll check on it today when we get back to Hollis," Meg said.

"I wish I wasn't saddling you with all the leg work. You have enough to do right now."

They had reached the end of the hall and were making their way back.

"I'd be happy to check for you. I think Dr. Coburg has moved here to Walton."

They fell silent for the rest of the trip to the end of the hall.

"So, were you able to find any fabric you could use?" he asked as they turned to walk back.

Meg was surprised he even remembered the fabric. "Yes. I took home several pieces. Mrs. Stuart came yesterday. We worked all day. You should see the pile. I don't know if we'll get it done in time, but we have to try. You probably won't be seeing much of me for the next few weeks, even if you're living in Hollis."

"That's fine. I need to concentrate on getting a job and strengthening my legs. Or I could just come over and pester you," Jack teased.

"You do that and I'll teach you how to sew and put you to work!" Meg was only half teasing. "You'd have to see the pile of projects to understand how deeply entrenched we are in this."

They'd reached the other end of the hall again. As they approached, Dr. Coburg walked by without even glancing their way.

"Last time I saw Dr. Coburg, Nellie had him in her clutches. Looks like Aunt Elaine is here and I have to go. I'll see you Friday. Be ready. You can ride with us back to Hollis." With a wave she hurried to the front of the hospital.

Aunt Elaine was, indeed, waiting for her and they left for home. Nellie talked the whole way regaling them about her conversation with Philip, how wonderful it was to see him, how happy he'd been to see her, and how he'd promised to eat lunch with her on Friday. Maybe he'd even take her to the diner near the hospital. She'd miss lunch with Phoebe and Sarah but she could hardly wait to spend time with Philip.

"Aunt Elaine," Meg interrupted Nellie as they drove into town. "Could you drop me off at the grocery instead of at home? It's not far to walk home from there."

They left Meg at the entrance. She waved as they drove off, then turned and entered the store. It was a smaller store than the ones in Walton, but they usually found what they needed or Mr. Miller would order it for them.

"How can I help you today, Meg?" Mr. Miller asked from behind the counter.

"I have a strange request. I know Dr. Coburg moved into Walton to work at the hospital. I was wondering if your room is available. I have a friend from the hospital, a soldier who was wounded. He's recovered enough to live on his own, but not enough to go home. He still needs to be under the care of the doctors at the hospital in Walton. He's also looking for a job. Is there any way you can help him?" Meg hesitated. Her speech had sounded so good when she'd worked out in her mind, but it didn't sound the same when she said it out loud. She flushed and waited for Mr. Miller to say something, anything. She didn't have to wait long.

"I take it you didn't see the sign in the window?" Mr. Miller asked, pointing.

Meg looked. A small "Help Wanted" sign hung in the window that hadn't been there the last time she'd been to the store.

"Put that up yesterday. You're the first to even ask about it. So, to answer your questions, yes, the room is available. And yes, he can have a job if he is willing to work. What day will he be moving here? What are the nature of his injuries? When can he start?"

"A new bunch of wounded soldiers will arrive on Friday. They are discharging Jack to make room for them. We'll be in Walton volunteering at the hospital on Friday and he'll come with us when we drive back. Jack's legs were burned by mustard gas in France. He couldn't walk when he returned but he's improved to the place he can walk with a cane."

Despite his gruff expression, Mr. Miller's eyes twinkled at her. "I'd love to help one of our soldiers get back on his feet – literally.

It's the least I can do. He can start first thing Monday. I'll make arrangements for wages and rent with the man himself when he arrives on Friday."

Her errand complete, Meg hurried home before it got dark, eager to share her news with Gran. Jack would be moving to Hollis on Friday.

Chapter Twenty-six

Friday, Meg could hardly wait to give Jack the good news. She hurried to his ward as soon as she arrived at the hospital, but found it occupied by men she didn't know, and who were just as sick as Jack had been when they'd first met.

She turned to leave the ward and saw Dr. Fulton approaching. He smiled when he saw Meg. "He's in the waiting room near the entrance. He said to tell you to look for him there, though I don't think he's expecting you until this afternoon."

Meg thanked the doctor, then hurried back the way she'd come. She found Jack in the waiting room where she'd met Nurse Rogers on the first day she'd volunteered, months ago. He was sitting in a chair, reading a book. One small suitcase contained all of his belongings. He looked up when she entered the room.

"Fancy seeing you here," he said with a grin. "Glad you found me. The soldiers came in early. They brought them up from Portland last night."

"I looked for you in the men's ward. Dr. Fulton told me you were waiting here.

"Everything is arranged. You can come and live at the grocery and Mr. Miller has a job for you. He'd put a Help Wanted sign in the window this week. Aunt Elaine has agreed to take you to Hollis with us this afternoon. I guess all you have to do is wait." Meg chuckled. "It's going to be a long day for you."

"Your news has already made the wait easier. I didn't even know if I had a place to live or a job when they kicked me out of my room. I'm glad this worked out."

"Can you at least come eat lunch with us? Then you don't have to sit alone all day in this little room."

"I'll happily eat lunch with you. Hey, would you like to go to the coffee shop? It would be fun to get outside, even though it's cold."

"That would be nice." A pleased smile spread across her face.

Jack responded with a grin of his own. "Until lunch."

"Until lunch," Meg said.

∞

The morning dragged as Meg listened to Nellie recount her activities of the day before. She was trying to figure out how to get or make a gown for the ball. Right now her plans were to remake an old dress. Aunt Elaine wasn't fond of the idea so Nellie was having to do all the work on it alone. She wanted Meg and Gran to help, but Meg reminded her of that large stack of fabric that needed to be sewn before the bazaar.

Nellie sighed "I wish you hadn't gotten all that fabric to sew."

"You could come and help," Meg suggested. "If we finish in time, I could help you with your dress."

"I'm no good at that sort of sewing. You could take a break one day to help me."

"I will if I have time, but don't count on it. It'll be a busy couple weeks." Meg turned back to the mending in her lap.

Nellie fell silent, lost in her own thoughts and plans.

Finally, lunch time arrived. Nellie had arranged to meet the doctor in the dining room.

The two girls left together. Meg went with Nellie to the dining room before she met Jack, hoping to thank the girls for telling her about the fabric. When they arrived at the dining room door, Nellie looked around the room. Dr. Coburg was already sitting at a table with Phoebe and Sarah. Nellie hurried across the room toward them. Meg followed.

"I see you found my friends!" Nellie exclaimed as she walked up.

"I've known these two for a while. We've worked together off and on for years," the doctor replied. "It's great that you already know each other." He waved his hand at the empty seat at the table but didn't stand. "We saved a seat. We're all on the clock, so we went ahead and started. We didn't save you a seat, Meg. You can pull up a chair from another table." He rose as if to fetch a chair himself but stopped when Meg shook her head.

"I have to meet Jack," she said, and excused herself. Meg watched Nellie turn crimson and, for the first time in months, she felt sympathy for the girl. She left Nellie to take her seat and try to fit in.

Meg joined Jack in the waiting room, then they walked to the diner where the girls had eaten the first day. They sat at a table near the door since the walk was long and tiring for Jack. Meg told him about what had happened back in the dining room. He shook his head.

"That's just rude. He set a time to meet her, got there early, then sat with two other girls. Not a very nice guy, you know?"

Meg had to agree. She couldn't understand why he would snub Nellie, but she refused to dwell on it and ruin this time with Jack.

"Tell me," Jack began once they had ordered their food and the waitress had brought it to the table, "what do you like about Hollis and Walton?"

"I love the ocean." Meg replied, without hesitation. "Of course I love my Gran and getting to be with her. But if you are talking about this place, like the place I live and not the people, it's the ocean."

"I still have a hard time with it. Seeing that great blue expanse brings back bad memories." Jack stated.

"What sort of memories?"

Jack hesitated. His gaze shifted to a point outside the window and his eyes darkened.

Meg laid her hand on his arm. "You don't have to talk about it, if it's too painful."

"They took me to a convent by the ocean in France when I was burned. I lay in my bed, waves of pain washing over me, just like the waves I could hear on the shore in the distance. Sometimes the waves crashed against the rocks. I imagined crashing against those same rocks. I imagined the pain ending. Forever. I cried and screamed like a madman and a weakling. The nuns told me not to. I couldn't stop myself. The screams came as though I wasn't in charge of my own body or faculties. They told me I was lucky. I'd walk again.

"I took a transport to England once I'd healed enough to travel. My commanding officer was on it with me. His legs had been blown off. He was blind. He told me I was lucky. That I'd walk again." Jack winced and looked down at the table. He covered her hand with his. "He died on the transport. Never even got back to England."

Meg listened. Tears slid, unchecked down her cheeks. She had no idea the depth of his pain.

"I've made you cry. Sorry about that."

Meg blinked. The Jack she knew had returned. She pulled a handkerchief from her purse and wiped her face.

"Please don't apologize. I want to hear you talk about it."

Jack gave a sardonic laugh. "You don't want to hear all of it."

"Why not?"

"I wish I didn't have the memories in the first place. Why would I share them with anyone else?"

"You can't bear them alone."

Sadness filled his eyes. He reached across the table and cupped her chin in his hand. "But I must."

"If you need to share the burden with me, you can. I can bear it with you." Meg covered his hand with hers and leaned into it.

Jack pulled away and looked out the window. Thoughts and emotions flickered over his face. "You know what the worst loss was?"

Meg watched Jack's face. His eyes squeezed shut, his lips twisted with pain. He didn't wait for her reply.

"I went to basic training with a guy named Sean Cavanaugh. Guy about my age. Taller than me. He didn't fit into the trenches. Had to walk around hunched over all the time. He carried around this picture of his wife and kid."

Jack pulled a faded picture from his coat pocket and laid it on the table between them. The edges were torn and ruffled as though they'd been wet for a long period of time. One long side was stained brown. With a gasp, Meg realized it wasn't dirt, it was blood. She jerked her gaze back to Jack's face, but he still stared out the diner window.

"We were so close to the final push. The last big battle. Everything went in our favor after that. Orders were to leave our trench and clear the enemy trench. We started before dawn. It was so dark, wet, cold. We hadn't gone a hundred feet when Cavanaugh was hit by an enemy bullet right in the leg. He bled out in a couple minutes. I got him back to our trench and tried to stop it, but it was too little, too late. I watched the life leave him, watched him take his last breath."

Jack drew a shuddering breath. "I see him in my dreams at night. Or I feel my legs burning again. Sometimes both together. Then I wake in a sweat and can't sleep anymore. He's still gone. My legs are healing."

When he met Meg's gaze again, he forced a smile onto his lips. "The worst of the pain is over. They were right. I can walk again. I shouldn't complain. I'm one of the lucky ones. But what about her?" He tapped the picture with his finger. "I wrote a letter to tell her he died a hero. It wasn't enough. I should have saved him. I should have died instead so he could go home to be with his family."

"It doesn't work that way." The words slipped out before Meg could stop them. "I wouldn't have ever met you if you had."

Jack's eyes searched her face. They were filled with pain. "It still isn't fair." He picked up the photo and regarded it for a long moment. Then he slid it into his coat pocket again. He took another deep breath.

Meg opened her mouth to say something but Jack stopped her with a raised finger. "I don't want to talk about it anymore. Tell me, why do you like the ocean?"

Meg ached for him. But the look on his face brooked no argument. She thought about the ocean, its changing colors and moods. A smile flickered across her face and her eyes looked at Jack without seeing him.

"It's beautiful and changing, and stretches as far as the eye can see. Sometimes it's dark green and brooding with white foam caps. Sometimes it's light blue and frolics across the sand. The waves come, one on top of the other. They never stop. But you don't want them to. You want to look at them forever. I love the feel of the sand in my toes. I love the smell of the water."

"You make it sound like a different ocean than the one I've known. You mentioned once that Hollis was walking distance from a beach. Is there any way we could go there sometime if we get a nice day? Maybe I haven't seen the ocean from the right perspective."

"I'd love that. There are many places in Hollis you'll like. I promise to show you around. We'll definitely visit the ocean."

"See, I miss Indiana," Jack said. "It's not like I couldn't stand to live anywhere else. But the smell of the earth, the sight of acres and acres of corn and wheat blowing in the wind, windmills dotting the landscape, well, it makes me homesick just thinking about it."

"It's like another version of the ocean," Meg said, her voice quiet, almost dreamy. "Wave after wave of foamy water scraping up on the beach or the rustle of acres and acres of corn or wheat as the wind blows across it, making it look like green or golden waves. Amber waves of grain and all that."

"I forget that you used to live there and you've seen it, too. Do you ever miss it?" he asked.

139

"I used to. But I fell in love with the ocean. The ocean was something stable. The constancy of it helped me through the loneliness and grief when I first got here."

$$\infty$$

They finished lunch and walked back to the hospital. When Meg arrived back in their little work room, Nellie was already there. She glanced up as Meg entered the room then put her head back down to work. Her eyes were ringed in red. She'd been crying. Meg felt genuine sympathy for her.

"It was unfair and wrong how he treated you at lunch," Meg said softly. "I'm so sorry."

"Oh, you left before anything happened. Turns out, he's been seeing the girls and doing things with them this whole time. They've been 'showing him around'. They even helped him find the boarding house he's renting now. I sat there the whole time while he ignored me. Well I'm done with him, too! Now I know why he was so eager to get away from Hollis and move here. He wanted to be with them more than me. Fine, he can have those tramps if he wants. See if I care." Nellie sobbed into a handkerchief clutched in her hand.

Meg slid an arm around her cousin's shoulders and let her cry. "If I'd have known they would treat you that way, I wouldn't have made plans with Jack. I thought I was doing you a favor by not coming along as an extra wheel. But you probably could have used the moral support."

"You knew, didn't you." Nellie was quieter now. Hurt radiated from her voice.

"Suspected. Didn't know," Meg answered. "Some things were curious about the whole situation. I had my concerns."

"Why didn't you say something and warn me?" Nellie cried.

"Nothing was certain. All I had was a suspicion. Besides, I'm pretty sure you wouldn't have listened. You would have accused me of being jealous." Meg answered as gently as she could.

Nellie hung her head. "I would have done that. I've thought you and everyone else were jealous of me because I had a doctor for a beau, but it turns out he isn't a beau at all, at least not to me."

"Let's get our work done and not think about him anymore. We have lots of other things we can talk about." But Meg knew they would talk of nothing else.

Chapter Twenty-seven

Jack rode with them to Hollis that evening. He and Aunt Elaine chatted in the front seat. Now and then, Meg interjected comments. Nellie sat in morose silence and stared out the window.

Meg helped Jack out of the car, led him inside the grocery store, and introduced him to Mr. Miller. Then the three women left him to discuss business with his new employer and get situated in his new rooms. Meg promised to look in on him the next day and invited him to eat supper with them whenever he wanted.

The next three weeks flew by for Meg and Gran. They worked hard to finish their projects for the bazaar. On the days Meg didn't volunteer, they sewed like their life depended on it. On volunteer days, Meg did the housework when she got home so Gran could keep working. Mrs. Stuart and Emily came over most days. Mrs. Stuart brought her machine over to Gran's house because there was more room and less distractions.

Little by little, the pile of unfinished projects diminished and the pile of finished items grew. Meg knitted her blanket every evening. Just as they began to feel there was no way to finish in time, they reached the bottom of the pile. All that remained was to put last minute touches on their crafts.

Frigid temperatures kept Meg from showing Jack around town. Turned out, she didn't have much spare time and neither did he as he learned his new job at the grocery.

Nellie was almost impossible to live with. She moped for a few days. Then she decided the girls in Walton had stolen Dr. Coburg from her and she needed to win him back. Meg gave up trying to talk sense into her.

A week before the bazaar and ball, Meg returned the fabric they hadn't used to the house Sarah had showed them a few weeks earlier. She left the hospital early and ventured into the crisp winter afternoon. A tall, somewhat familiar gentleman answered the door when she rang the bell. To her surprise she recognized Dr. Fulton, who had treated Jack.

"Oh, hello!" she exclaimed. "I'm here to drop off some fabric we had leftover."

"Please come in. You'll need to talk to my wife. She's in the sun room. I'm certain she'd be happy for the distraction. That poor lady hasn't taken a break from sewing in days." The doctor stepped aside so Meg could enter, then led the way through the house to a bright room overlooking a garden.

The lady in question looked up from her sewing machine and was surprised to see Meg. "Come in and sit with me a moment," she begged. "My neck and shoulders need me to take a rest from the machine. What brings you by today?"

"I'm returning the leftover fabric like you requested. Also, I have a quilt and a blanket to enter in the silent auction, if it is still open."

"Of course, of course! How wonderful! I'm amazed how much you used. I can hardly wait to see how much we raise this year for the hospital from all this material. Bring the blankets over the day or two before so we can have them displayed when people arrive that morning. Are you planning to attend the ball afterward?"

It was a surprising change in subject and Meg felt herself blush. "I wasn't planning to. It would be nice, but… it's just Gran and me. I don't have a dress to wear and, well, I don't know...." her voice faded as she ran out of excuses.

"Have you ever been to one before?" Mrs. Fulton asked.

"Oh, no." Meg smiled. "It's okay, though. After all the work we've been doing, it'll be a treat to go home and not have a pile of projects awaiting me. I can't stay. My aunt will be along to take us home. Thank you so much for inviting me in. I'm thankful to warm up before the ride home."

Meg rose to go and followed Mrs. Fulton to the door.

"I will see you next week," Mrs. Fulton said.

Meg smiled and waved as she hurried up the street and back to the hospital.

∞

Jack came for supper that evening. After their meal he admired the blanket Meg had finished the evening before. Then he got a progress report on the sewing projects from Gran.

He chuckled. "I almost feel like I'm a part of this. I'm so nervous about whether or not you will finish in time."

"We'll finish," Gran said, not a trace of doubt in her tone. "We can complete what we have left with no trouble."

A week earlier, Meg wouldn't have shared Gran's confidence. But now, as she looked at the small details that remained, she agreed.

"Are you going to stay for the ball?" Jack asked Meg. "I'm thinking about seeing if I can ride with you into Walton and be there for the day, but I'd need to be prepared to stay for the evening if you are."

"They're having a ball?" said Gran, surprised.

"Yes. Meg didn't tell you?"

"She hasn't said a word about it."

"I wasn't going to stay," Meg said without looking up from her work.

"Why ever not?" Gran asked.

"It will be a long day and you'll be tired for one thing. For another thing, it costs money to attend. And I don't have anything to wear."

"You're young. You'll still have enough energy for it," Gran said. "I'm sure we can find something for you to wear."

$$\infty$$

"Follow me," Gran said the next morning as soon as they'd finished breakfast.

She led the way to the attic. The low attic ceiling followed the pitch of the roof and neither Gran nor Meg could stand upright. Weak sunlight filtered through small windows on either end. The space was empty save for a few old pieces of furniture, the Christmas decorations, some old, empty trunks, a couple boxes, and a dress form.

Gran retrieved one of the boxes. She brushed away the thick dust that covered the top, revealing gold lettering. Meg read the name of a dress maker's shop in Portland. Gran handed the box to Meg and the two women made their way down the narrow attic steps to Meg's room.

Meg set the box on her desk and removed the lid. Inside, she saw deep blue silk, lace, and fabric flowers. Gran grasped the fabric and lifted it out of the box.

The vintage dress was made in a style popular forty years earlier with a princess neckline and a V at the waist. The large, poofy sleeves went to the elbow, followed by deep lace with a row of rosettes sewed where the lace met the sleeves. The same rosettes were at the point of the neckline and clustered to one side at the waist. The back had a beautiful cascading bustle with the same deep lace.

"I wore this dress to the last ball I attended with your grandpa," Gran said. "We could remake it so it looks more modern, but I think it will fit you. You'll have to wear this underneath." She pulled a corset from the bottom of the box. "I'm amazed it's still in such good shape. I haven't taken it out in years."

"We shouldn't change anything about it. It's beautiful and unique just like it is," Meg said. She took the dress from Gran and held it up to herself in front of the mirror. She'd always thought herself plain with her brown eyes and brown hair. The navy dress brought life and color to her cheeks. It made her feel pretty.

"Let me help you try it on," Gran said. She gathered the dress from Meg and draped it over the bed. Meg slipped out of the dress she was wearing. Gran helped Meg tighten the corset. Meg stepped into the dress and lifted it up and onto her arms. Gran used a button hook to fasten it closed. It fit perfectly.

"You look beautiful." Gran gave Meg a teary smile and wiped the corner of her eye with her handkerchief. "You have to go to the ball. We'll figure out a way to get you there."

$$\infty$$

When Meg and Nellie got to the hospital the next morning, Dr. Fulton and his wife were waiting for them.

"My husband has told me what a help you girls have been around this hospital. You make it easier for the Ladies Aid. It would be our honor to sponsor you girls to come to the ball. It's a small way to thank you for all you have done." Mrs. Fulton looked at Meg.

"Yes! Yes! Of course!" Nellie answered for them. She clapped her hands and beamed at the doctor and his wife. Then her face fell "But I don't think Meg will be able to come. She cares for our grandmother and will need to get home to her."

Mrs. Fulton's gaze had never left Meg's face. "Is this true? Could your Gran get by without you for one evening?" she asked.

"Gran was hoping to find a way I could stay for the ball. She even found a dress I could wear. I'll need to make arrangements for her to get home after the bazaar, but I think she'll want me to attend. Thank you so much for the opportunity."

146

Meg managed to keep the extent of her response to the smile she couldn't wipe off her face. She hugged Mrs. Fulton, then hurried to the sewing room to get to work. On the inside, she was jumping up and down with excitement. She could hardly wait to tell Gran and Jack the good news.

Chapter Twenty-eight

The day of the bazaar Meg woke before dawn. She didn't want to crawl out from under her warm blankets into the cold room. They'd stayed late the night before setting up tables for the bazaar and finishing last minute details at home. She was tired.

By the time early morning sunshine pierced the cold morning air, Aunt Elaine arrived and they were ready to leave. Gran and Emily Stuart were riding to Walton with them. Jack planned to ride over later in the day with Dr. and Mrs. Grey.

They arrived at the hall they'd decorated the day before in time to set their items out on the table before people began trickling in. A steady stream of them came by their table all day long. Gran's apple preserves were famous throughout the region. Some people came just for those. Before Meg could believe it was possible, an official came by their table to inform them closing time had come and they could pack away the rest of their goods. The preserves had been gone for a long time. Only a few items remained. They put those in boxes for storage until the bazaar next year.

∞

"Looks like the whole town decided to drive to the bazaar today. And most of Hollis, too," Dr. Grey griped as he drove up and down looking for a place to park the car.

"You should pull in there next to the library," Mrs. Grey said. She patted her husband's arm and pointed at the spot. "They're closed today so I'm sure they won't mind."

"It's a hike to get to the hall from here." Dr. Grey cut a significant look over his shoulder at Jack.

Jack collected his cane and prepared to get out of the car. He began working his legs to loosen them up after the car ride. "Don't mind me. I'm told walking will aid in my recovery."

Dr. Grey chuckled and pulled into the one empty spot on the whole road. "That's the spirit."

The sunlight had done little to warm the air. Jack tugged his coat tighter around him and pulled the scarf Meg had given him over his mouth. Each step could be treacherous in this cold. He tried to walk where he was sure he'd get traction.

The hall felt stuffy. Jack shrugged off the scarf and tucked it in his pocket. He waited for his eyes to adjust to the lighting. The bustling room came into view. Tables rimmed the room and patrons moved from table to table. He managed to locate Gran's table in the midst of a crowd of people and moved that direction. Emily Stuart took his money when he bought a jar of apple butter and an apron for his mom. He waved at Gran and moved to the next table.

Jack's eyes scanned the room for a certain brown head he wanted to see, with no success. He glanced at the contents of the tables he passed. What did a bachelor like himself need with any of these things? One man had tooled leather belts and wallets. He bought a wallet for his dad.

The crowd, with all their laughter and conversation, flowed around him. Jack felt apart from all of it. He saw other soldiers in groups or with their girl on their arm. His eyes scanned for that brown, curly head once more. Still nothing.

Jack found himself at the front of the hall admiring the items people had taken a long time to create. Gran's quilt was stunning. She claimed uneven stitches and mismatched seams, but his unskilled eyes couldn't see them. A painting depicted a wooded hill with a glimpse of the ocean in the distance and a lighthouse on a point jutting out into it. It was breathtaking but not what Jack had in mind.

There it was on the end, draped over a stand. Two men in uniform stood in front of it. One of them ran their hand over the even stitches.

"It's pretty, but too heavy for my taste," the taller one said.

"Too heavy? In this weather? You've got to be kidding." The shorter, stockier one ran his hand over the blanket again. "I'm thinking about bidding on it. It'll keep me warm until I get home to my girl."

"You could pick one in a color you want at that table over there. Probably for a lot less, too."

"Yeah," the shorter soldier hesitated and looked at the table his friend had indicated. "Guess I'll see what they have before I bid on this one." The two men walked away.

Jack frowned and fingered the money in his pocket. He looked at the things he'd already bought and wondered if he should have bid first. In his mind's eye, he could see that brown, curly head bent over the stitches he saw before him now. Her fingers flew and the blanket grew as he watched. She'd knitted and purled and cabled a masterpiece and he couldn't abide the thought of someone else winning it. Wrapping in it would be as if he was wrapped in her arms.

Jack shook away the thought. He pulled the final pay he'd gotten from the army out of his pocket and counted it once more. He was working for Mr. Miller now and his new employer had been more than fair with his wages. Jack could spare a bit more than he'd first thought to ensure he'd get Meg's blanket. He stepped to the box beside the stand, wrote his bid and his name on the paper, and stuffed them inside the box before he could change his mind.

His stomach thrilled with excitement and nerves. He only hoped it was enough.

He took a couple coins and bought popcorn and deer jerky from a vendor. The popcorn was soggy and the jerky was tough but he didn't mind. He scanned the crowd for that brown head one more time. He thought he caught sight of her bending over their table but lost sight of her again the next moment. It didn't matter. He'd see her tonight.

"Are you enjoying yourself?"

Dr. Fulton's voice startled Jack out of his reverie. He looked around at the older man and nodded. "It's quite the event," he said.

"They'll start planning for next year on Monday," Dr. Fulton said. "People come in from miles away for this event every year."

"It's impressive," Jack said, "especially in the middle of winter."

"Do you plan on dancing this evening?"

"I'm going to give it my best try." Jack tapped the cane. "If I can't find a girl to lean on, maybe I'll use this."

Dr. Fulton chuckled and patted Jack's back. "I'm sure you'll find a girl."

But as Jack considered how much trouble he was having locating the girl he wanted to dance with tonight, he decided he couldn't share Dr. Fulton's confidence. He might have to resort to dancing with his cane Charlie Chaplin style.

The auction pieces were displayed at the front of the hall, including Meg's blanket, Gran's quilt, some intricate embroidery, knitted lace, wood carvings, and a painting. All day people had been coming by and placing bids into boxes next to each item. Once all the tables had been emptied and cleared away, everyone turned their attention to the front of the hall to see who had won. So many people stayed that Gran, Emily, and Meg crowded into a corner at the back of the room and waited. Three men sorted the bids to determine whose was the highest for each item.

The painting would be last, of course. Meg wondered who had painted such a beautiful landscape. Gran's quilt went first to one of the bankers in town. His wife was ecstatic. The embroidery went next to one of the nurses.

Her blanket went next. They were too far back to hear the names being called so Meg was more than surprised when a tall, sandy-haired soldier in uniform stood to claim it. He limped to the front using a cane for support. It was Jack. The rest of the world faded into the background as she watched him collect the blanket and turn back to the room. He looked for her, but couldn't find her in the crowd. In a way, Meg was thankful he couldn't. He didn't even try to hide his pleasure as he carried the blanket from the platform. She lost sight of him in the mass of people.

The room cleared once the day's events concluded. Meg and Nellie rode with Dr. and Mrs. Fulton to their house to dress. They would chaperone the two young women to the ball that evening. Aunt Elaine drove Gran and Emily back to Hollis.

Meg's stomach fluttered with nervous excitement as they dressed in the Fulton's guest room. She imagined tripping over her dress or her hair coming unpinned. She didn't need to worry. Mrs. Fulton knew what she was doing.

She seated each girl in turn before the mirror at her dressing table. With deft movements, she secured their curls to the top of their heads, then pinned flowers into the girls' hair. They all swept downstairs to the Fulton's sitting room.

"I haven't had this much fun in years," Mrs. Fulton said. "Not since my girls grew up and left home." She stepped back to survey her work. "You both look beautiful."

"I have to agree, my dear," the doctor said from his seat by the fire. He smiled over the top of the paper he was reading at the two nervous young women standing before him. "This idea of yours was a good one."

Meg didn't know what to do with herself once they were ready for the ball. She paced the sitting room floor.

"Come, sit with me." Mrs. Fulton patted the settee next to her.

"I'll crush my dress," Meg said. She twisted her fingers together.

"Your dress will be fine. Here, a cup of tea and a bit of cake will invigorate and calm you." She handed the cup she'd poured to Meg and patted the seat next to her again. "Sit. You'll wear a hole in my rug with your pacing."

"You'll use all your energy pacing and have none left for dancing," said Dr. Fulton. His eyes twinkled at her.

Meg laughed and perched on the edge of the settee. She took the offered tea and sipped. Her foot bounced up and down of its own accord.

"Do you plan on dancing this evening, Mrs. Fulton?" Nellie asked.

"I might enjoy a waltz or two with my husband. What about you?"

"I believe there is a certain doctor she has her eye on," Dr Fulton teased.

Meg's eyes widened at Nellie over the top of her cup and Nellie flushed.

Dr. Fulton turned his gaze back to Meg. "I think we all know with whom our dear Meg is hoping to spend the evening."

"Dr. Fulton!" Mrs. Fulton wagged her finger at her husband. "Quit your teasing!"

Despite her embarrassment, Meg laughed. "I suppose Walton isn't as big a city as we like to think, is it? The gossip still gets around."

"It gets around the hospital anyway," said Mrs. Fulton.

They braved the frigid night air to drive back to the hall. Meg marveled at the changes the Ladies Aid had wrought in the intervening hours. Tables full of refreshments waited on one side. The small orchestra tuned their instruments and warmed up in the front of the room.

People trickled into the hall. Meg discovered she wasn't the only one wearing vintage clothing. Three of the women wore Civil War era dresses complete with hoop skirts. She looked down at her dark blue silk and adjusted the ruffles and bustle. She still didn't dare sit for fear of crushing the lace and silk in the back.

Nellie stood in a cluster of nurses across the room. Meg started toward them. Out of the corner of her eye, she saw Dr. and Mrs. Grey enter the hall. Behind them limped a tall, handsome soldier in full dress uniform. His halting steps and proficient use of a cane belied the fact that not two months ago he couldn't even stand. Yet, here he was, the most handsome man in the room. His eyes met hers. He smiled. For several seconds, everything else faded to the background. They were the only people in the whole world.

The orchestra played the opening notes for the first waltz. Jack met her partway across the room. Meg barely registered that she'd been walking toward him.

"You look so handsome in your uniform," Meg said.

"There aren't even words for how beautiful you look tonight," Jack murmured close to her ear. "I hate to assume anything, so can I have this first dance?" He offered his hand.

Meg slipped her hand into his. "Of course."

He led her onto the floor, hooked his cane on his arm, bowed while she curtsied, then he drew her closer and settled his other arm around her waist. Jack's steps jerked and halted as he limped his way through the dance. He gripped Meg for support, but she didn't mind. They stayed at the edge of the dance floor.

"I never did see you earlier today," Jack said after they'd been dancing for a few minutes. "I looked for you, but you must have been busy."

"We had a steady stream of people at our table all day," Meg said. "I stepped away once to run an errand for Gran. Did you stop by the table for anything?"

"I bought some apple butter and one of those aprons for my mom."

"We could have given you both of those and saved you the money. Same with the blanket."

Jack shrugged. "It went to a good cause. Now, on these cold winter nights, I can wrap in my girl's showpiece and stay warm."

His face was close to hers. Meg didn't try to pull away. "Your girl. I like that."

"I went to France and got burned to get a girl. For the first time, I can see how I'm one of the lucky ones."

His eyes held hers. Meg's breath caught.

Then the music ended and the dancing stopped. All the dancers clapped, and searched out their next partner as the first strains of the next song began. Meg felt as if everything moved in slow motion around her. She caught a glimpse of Dr. Fulton approaching.

"I think I'll need to pace myself this evening," Jack said. His gaze still held hers but his hand left her back. He lifted her fingers to his lips.

"I hope you don't mind me claiming Miss Hollister for the next dance."

Jack's eyes never left Meg's. "I need to sit for a few minutes anyway. My stamina is nowhere near what it used to be."

Jack danced with Meg as much as he could that evening. When he tired, they fixed plates refreshments and found a place to sit and eat. They watched the dancers and talked about home and family. Jack told boyhood stories of trouble he'd gotten into with his brothers. Meg shared stories about growing up in a college town where her father was a professor, with football games and all night study sessions hosted by her parents.

Dr. and Mrs. Grey found them there when the dancing finished and the ballroom was emptying. Meg pulled Jack to his feet and they went in search of their coats.

Jack, Meg and Nellie rode home with Dr. and Mrs. Grey. Meg nestled close to Jack in the back seat. He held her hand. She let him. She was so tired, she could have laid her head on his shoulder and fallen asleep. Nellie stared out her own window in silence.

The Greys pulled to a stop in front of Gran's house and Jack walked her to the door. Light from a half moon and a sky full of stars glinted off the snow. The icy air stabbed their lungs and made Meg shiver. Despite the cold, Meg didn't want the evening to end.

"Thank you for a wonderful time," Meg said. Her words came out with puffs of smoke.

"It was a pleasure," Jack said in a near whisper.

"Goodnight." Meg turned to enter the house.

Jack caught her hand and stepped toward her again. For a moment they regarded each other in the moonlight. Jack ran the blade of his finger across her cheek. "Goodnight," he whispered back. Then he turned and walked back to the car.

Meg entered the house and the Greys drove up the street toward town.

Meg felt a strange sensation in the pit of her stomach - relief mixed with what could only be described as disappointment, though how one could feel both at the same time was beyond her. She felt certain Jack had considered kissing her, but decided not to do it.

Meg slipped off her shoes and tiptoed upstairs. She managed to unbutton all the tiny buttons on the back of the navy dress and step out of it. She draped it over the desk, then pulled her nightgown over her head and climbed into bed.

But as tired as she was it was hours before she was able to fall asleep.

$$\infty$$

"It was a horrible evening." Nellie stalked into the living room after dinner and flopped onto the couch. Meg sighed and picked up her knitting. She'd been hoping for a quiet Sunday afternoon, but she supposed that wasn't to be.

"I wish I hadn't let myself get talked into staying," Nellie continued. "I wasn't planning on it in the first place, you know. But when the doctor offered I felt I had to say yes."

Meg glared at Nellie's profile. She'd been planning on attending one way or other. Meg bit back an angry comment but Nellie was still talking.

"Philip brought Sarah and then spent the whole evening with her. I think she has him under a spell or something. He didn't dance with anyone else all evening. I saw him look at me a couple times and his eyes told me everything. He didn't want to be with her. He wanted to be with me.

"I've got it all worked out. I'm going to start winning him back tomorrow when we go to Walton to volunteer."

Gran sat by the window and had heard the entire soliloquy. Nellie stopped to take a breath and Gran spoke, stopping Nellie's further comments before they began.

"There is no way you believe everything that is coming out of your own mouth. Regardless, it isn't true. If a man comes to a party with a particular woman, if he spends most of the evening with her, if he almost never even looks at another woman, you can assume that he is interested in her romantically. If there is another woman there, and no matter how nice she looks he ignores her, it is because he is *not* interested in her romantically.

"You are a silly foolish girl for throwing yourself at a man who has no interest in you. You should be embarrassed."

Nellie's head whipped back as if she'd been struck. A look of horror covered her face. She jerked to her feet.

"I don't care if you are my Grandmother you have no right to talk to me that way," she said with a toss of her head.

"Someone had to say it. You won't listen to Meg who has to put up with your nonsense all the time. You won't even listen to your own mother."

Nellie strutted across the room, yanked her coat off the hook, and shrugged it on. "I'm not going to stay here and take this. I don't see how fighting for my man is a problem."

"Nellie!" Meg cried. She'd listened in stunned silence to their exchange. Now she stood and crossed to Nellie. "Remember the day that you were to meet Dr. Coburg for lunch and when you got there, not only had he already started eating lunch, but he was sitting with several other nurses? You were convinced then that he wasn't the man for you. You told me that you wished I'd have said something sooner so you wouldn't have been so embarrassed at the time. Now we're saying something. We're trying to save you from embarrassing yourself again. You watch. In only a few weeks we'll find that he is engaged to Sarah."

"No." Nellie shook her head as she shoved her hands into her gloves. "You are both wrong. You'll see." She marched out of the house, slamming the door behind her.

Meg sank onto her chair and dropped her face into her hands. A soft moan of frustration escaped her. Gran sagged in her chair by the window.

"I shouldn't have said anything," Gran said. "It was unwise of me." She lifted the lace curtain aside and watched Nellie stalk up the street.

"Gran, someone had to say something. I've already tried. She won't listen to me. I didn't pay attention to her at all last night. I didn't notice if she was having a good time or not. I was so wrapped up in being with Jack I didn't notice anything else. How selfish is that?"

"It isn't your job to make sure she has a good time, Meg. She's a grown woman. She needs to act like one."

Bright winter sunlight and warmer temperatures beckoned. The fresh air would feel wonderful. Meg felt stifled after that exchange. "I think I'll take that walk I was considering earlier."

"Gran," she asked as she pulled on her own coat and gloves, "am I imagining Jack's interest in me?"

"No, my dear, I don't think you are. Now go enjoy the beautiful day and try not to think about it."

Meg stepped outside into the bracing cold air. She turned toward town, then changed her mind and struck off into the woods. The snow wasn't as deep there. She wanted to be alone with her thoughts.

No matter how hard she tried, she couldn't think of a way to mend things with Nellie. Maybe this was something Nellie needed to work through on her own.

Nellie refused to volunteer in Walton. She wouldn't speak to Meg or Gran. Aunt Elaine drove Meg to the hospital a few times. Word reached them from Uncle Daniel that the worst of the sickness was over. The women weren't needed at the hospital. Aunt Elaine decided not to go any more.

Meg rode to Walton with Dr. Grey on those rare occasions he needed to go. She was surprised how much she missed the routine of her thrice weekly trips. They'd always tell her how much they missed her. She helped as much as she could. But it wasn't the same. They didn't need as much extra help as they had before. Some days she felt like they were struggling to find things for her to do so Meg stopped going.

Gossip being what it is, word got around that Dr. Coburg was courting a certain young lady who worked at the hospital. Because of hospital rules, she'd been forced to quit her job. The news didn't surprise Meg at all. It hadn't surprised Nurse Rogers, either. Meg felt heartsick for Nellie, but there wasn't much she could do. Nellie had completely cut them out of her life.

Chapter Twenty-nine

Jack improved every day. Dr. Grey was overjoyed at his progress and insisted that he would be well by spring. Meg was happy for him, but she was sad as well, a fact she kept to herself.

The weather warmed for a week or two. Much of the snow melted. The roads turned into a muddy mess. Then they got another heavy snow storm. Meg and the Stuart girls made the trek over to the Big Hill to go sledding with instructions to stay clear of all trees. Penny, still not fully healed, stayed home. She watched their departure from their front room window, tears slipping down her cheeks at the injustice of it all.

Jack was waiting when they got there. "I knew you'd come!" he shouted as soon as he saw them. "This is great! I've been dying to give this hill a try ever since I saw it!"

"You're kidding, right?" Emily was incredulous. "There is no way you'll be able to get back up with that cane."

"Watch me, kiddo." Jack took Emily's sled from her, set it on the ground, and dropped onto it. With a whoop and a holler he shoved off and flew down the hill.

"You shouldn't have challenged him like that," Meg said with an exasperated sigh. She seated herself on her own sled, arranged her skirts, and followed him. He'd need help getting up off the ground and climbing the hill.

It did prove to be more than he'd expected, but that didn't stop him from going down over and over again. He'd fight his way back up the hill while the rest took more than one trip. His legs were stiff.

He'd fall off the sled. Then he'd wait for someone to come down and help him up.

Meg relaxed and enjoyed herself. She'd hurry to the top and help the little girls get on their sled. Then she'd fly down on her own. She'd wait for Jack to take a trip down the hill so she could help him back to the top.

On his last trip down the hill, Jack struggled to stand at all. Meg was tired from all her trips up and down. She barely had the strength to pull Jack to his feet. His legs gave out and he landed with a plunk back on the ground, taking Meg down with him. She struggled to stand, but couldn't manage it.

"Aren't we the pair?" Jack said. He started laughing. "I'm already a cripple and we've all worn you out to the point you can't stand." He laughed harder.

Meg laughed along with him as she pushed herself to stand up. "I can't leave you here. Come on." She grabbed his hand and pulled. Nothing happened.

"I'm trying, I promise," Jack said around his chuckles. The more they struggled, the harder they laughed.

Finally, weak with laughter, Meg collapsed on the snowy ground next to Jack.

Meg took several deep breaths and got her laughter under control. Jack's subsided to chuckles. She stood and took his hand. At that moment, Emily Stuart yelled a warning too late. Her sled flew by, clipping Meg and sending her with a shriek onto the ground – and back into gales of laughter.

"I give up!" Meg gasped between fits of laughter. "I think I'll lie here for a minute and catch my breath!"

They hiked home, tired but happy, and piled into Gran's kitchen. She had prepared coffee, hot chocolate and fresh warm bread. Everyone had a much needed snack. Then the Stuarts went home, leaving Jack sitting at the table with Meg and Gran.

"I haven't had that much fun in a long time," Jack said with a grin and a contented, tired sigh.

"I thought you were crazy the first time you went down," Meg said. "It seemed like your mind was willing, but your flesh was weak. I'm glad I was wrong. Good job!"

"Yep, it's one more milestone. Couldn't have done that a month ago." Jack grinned even bigger. "I'll pay for it tomorrow. Still, being able to sled down that hill is worth it." He looked down at his soaked pant legs. Blood seeped through the fabric where the scar tissue had torn. That would take time to heal.

"So what happens once the doctor clears you?" Gran asked the question that Meg had been secretly wondering for a long time.

Jack grew serious. "I don't know. I hadn't thought that far ahead. I know I could stay here and work, but stocking grocery shelves isn't really what I want to do with the rest of my life."

"I can understand that," Gran said. "What do you want to do with it?"

"My dad has a farm. I've always loved helping him run it. I've been writing them. Dad said if I'm well enough by spring, he could use help with the planting and harvest this year. I'm thinking about it. But, I have reasons to consider staying here, too." Jack looked at Meg as he spoke.

She flushed and stood to put her cup and plate in the sink, hoping he hadn't seen. Her heart sank. Jack would be leaving. Now she wished she didn't know what his plans were. She wished they could go back to the way it had been earlier in the evening, when she'd been so happy, when they'd been having so much fun together.

Jack would be leaving. Meg wanted to cry. She fought back the tears that threatened despite her best efforts to keep them under control. She couldn't bring herself to look at him again. Instead, she busied herself with washing the dishes in the sink.

"It won't be for a while yet," Jack continued. "Dr. Grey is hoping I gain better mobility. I still have trouble sitting down, then standing back up. I wouldn't have been able to sled at all today, if Meg and the Stuart girls hadn't been there to help me."

"We'll miss you when you go," Gran said. She patted his hand. "It's getting late. I'd better get the fire stirred in the front room so we don't freeze to death tonight." Gran left the two young people in the kitchen.

Jack came and leaned against the counter next to Meg. "I've been wanting to talk with you about my plans for a while. It's never seemed like the right time. I'm not sure now was, either. Nothing like ruining a wonderful afternoon with bad news. I don't have to go, you know."

"I know. I almost wish you wouldn't. But I don't want you to stay here, stuck in a job that doesn't pay well and that you don't enjoy, all the while knowing your parents need you to make a living." Meg shook her head. "No, I can't ask you to stay here with all those things to consider."

"Meg." Jack touched her arm. "I like being with you, doing things with you, talking to you and listening to you. I'd rather be with you than anyone else in the whole world."

Meg looked up at him and placed her fingers on his mouth to stop him from saying more. "You need to get back to your room before it gets any colder. In a day or two, when the shock of it has worn off, I'll be okay."

"We can write letters."

"You'll be really busy."

"You can write me, then. I might go nuts if I don't hear from you."

Jack pulled Meg against his chest. She wrapped her arms around him and clung to him. He wasn't as thin as he had been at Christmas. His chest had filled out. She felt like she was losing him like she'd lost everyone else that mattered to her except Gran.

That night Meg cried herself to sleep.

Chapter Thirty

Meg was in love.

She realized this fact the night Jack told them his plans. Her heart ached with the thought of losing him in a few months, but there was nothing she could do about it. He'd leave. He'd forget all about her. There would be a girl back home in Indiana. She didn't know whether to try to wring all the enjoyment she could out of their remaining time together or push him away so losing him wouldn't hurt as much.

Jack didn't make it any easier for her. He came around more the next few weeks. He was there almost every evening for supper. Gran insisted on it and fixed things she knew he liked.

She thought maybe he loved her, too. Sometimes he'd bring her little things – a small box of heart shaped candy at Valentines day; the first crocuses that peeked above the snow; a single rose bud that he'd gotten somewhere. But now that he was choosing to leave over choosing to stay, she didn't know if he really loved her or if he brought the gifts because he was feeling sorry for her.

One beautiful evening in March, a soft wind blew the sweet smell of wet earth and new grass. Meg lingered on the back step after she dumped the dishwater. She'd been avoiding Jack for weeks. She made sure all their interaction took place with other people present.

She took another deep breath of the fragrant spring air then turned to go inside. Jack filled the doorway, blocking her way.

"You're avoiding me," he said.

164

Meg sighed and swung back around to look at the sunset. She sat down with a thump on the back step. "I'm not avoiding you." She twisted and looked up at him.

He stepped down and then, with effort, lowered himself onto the step beside her. "Then please tell me what's going on," he begged.

Meg watched the sky turn from blue to pink. She considered what to tell him and then decided to be direct. "I'm bracing myself for when you leave. It's going to hurt so much to lose you, to not have you around every day anymore." She looked at the ground. "I'm being silly about the whole thing. You need to go and help your dad. I have no hold on you, no right to even ask you to stay here."

Jack gave a relieved chuckle. He took a deep breath. He'd been holding his breath afraid she was hiding something serious. His entire body sagged with relief.

He glanced at Meg out of the corner of his eye. "You are *not* silly. As for having a hold on me, well," he hesitated, "You've had a hold on me from the first day we met. I was ready to *beg* you to come back and visit after that first day. I was so relieved that you were willing to come see me of your own accord."

It was Meg's turn to chuckle. She bumped his shoulder with hers. "You did look pretty pitiful that day," she said. "A girl would have had to be hard hearted to resist a fellow as pitiful as you."

"Hey, be careful now!" He grinned and bumped her shoulder in return. Then he grew serious. "I remember telling you a while back that a man who was interested in a girl would do anything he could to stay with her. You are probably thinking of that right now, aren't you? It's been niggling at me ever since I told you I was leaving. I keep imagining you think I'm leaving to get away from you. Is that a pretty close guess?"

Meg looked away so he couldn't see the tears that had formed in her eyes. That was exactly what she'd been thinking.

"Meg, please look at me."

She shook her head and tried to collect herself. After a moment she was able to face him.

"Is that how I've hurt you? By making you think I wanted to get away from you?" His intense eyes held hers.

"I couldn't figure out what I'd done to make you want to get away. Everything has been playing through my mind over and over, but I couldn't think of anything." Meg stifled a sob.

"You haven't done anything. Nothing. I'm not trying to get away from you. From the bottom of my heart, I wish I could stay. When my brother goes to college, Dad will be alone on the farm. My brother will be there for the planting this spring, but not for the harvest. They can't live if they don't plant and harvest. Dad can't do it alone. I feel this huge weight of responsibility for the place. I'm torn. With all my heart, I want to be here. At the same time, I feel like I need to be there. It's something I've never felt before. Am I making any sense at all?"

"Yes, you are, perfect sense." Meg met Jack's intense gaze for an instant then shifted hers to her fingers. She felt like he was seeing her very thoughts. Maybe he could. There had been many times he'd said something she'd been thinking.

As she sat there fidgeting with her fingers, a contented peace settled over her in place of the hurt and worry of the last few weeks. Jack reached over, stilled her hands, and took them in his own.

Meg leaned against him. "I'm going to miss you so much," she whispered. A tear slid down her cheek and dripped onto their joined hands.

"Not as much as I'll miss you," he whispered back.

Meg looked up at him. His face was so close. She could feel his breath on her cheek. He leaned toward her.

The back door opened and light from the kitchen spilled into the dusk. "Meg, where did you put those cookies you made yesterday? This boy is looking thin. I'm starting to feel thick so I thought we could send them with him."

Gran's timing couldn't have been worse.

Meg stood and turned to go into the house. Jack gripped her hand and tugged her back to the step. She shook her head with a smile, then followed Gran into the house to find the cookies for Jack. For the first time in weeks, she felt happy. They could cram the next weeks as full as possible to hold them through until they could be together again.

Chapter Thirty-one

"You're making great progress," Dr. Grey told Jack one afternoon in late March. "Keep it up and I'll be able to release you in a couple weeks. How are the nightmares?"

Jack's head jerked up. "How do you know about those?"

"You aren't the first or only injured soldier I've treated. The nightmares are common in those who've seen action."

Jack gripped the back of his neck with both hands and looked up at the ceiling. "I have them. Almost every night. Most of the time I can deal with what happens but sometimes I wake myself up screaming."

"What are you dreaming?"

"My last day of combat a fellow who'd been with me since basic got shot in the leg and died in my arms. I replay his death over and over in slow motion. We were weeks away from the war's finish. Why did he have to die then? He left a wife and a baby." Jack rubbed his face with a hand and swallowed against the tightness in the back of his throat. He coughed and cleared his throat then continued.

"The other thing I dream is that I'm back in the convent in France and it feels like my legs are on fire again. That's the one wakes me up screaming. I wake up and discover they aren't burning anymore." Jack rested his elbows on his knees. "Do the nightmares ever stop?"

"I don't know. I've never met anyone who got rid of them completely. But I've read that they improve over time. Have you told anyone aside from me about those last days of combat?"

Jack thought about the many conversations he'd had with Meg. He'd told her some of the painful memories, but not all of them. "It's hard to talk about them."

"You need to try. It might help."

"I've told Meg some of it. Hate to burden her, though."

"She's a strong young woman, more than capable of handling this."

"Yes, she is."

"Does she know you're planning to return to Indiana in time for planting?"

"I told her. She took the news about as well as could be expected. Thing is, I'd like to ask her to marry me before I go, but I don't have a ring or token to leave with her. Any suggestions about where I'd get one?"

Dr. Grey beamed at Jack.

"You can't say a word to her about it," Jack warned.

"I'd never do any such thing." Dr. Grey patted Jack's arm. "I might be able to help you with that, if you can get a morning off one of these weeks. I still drive up to Walton once a week to check in at the hospital. You could look around at the shops while I'm at the hospital. I can recommend a couple shops if needed. Talk to Miller. I'll bet he'll give you a couple hours if you ask."

Tuesday mornings were slow, and that happened to be the day Dr. Grey went to Walton. Jack made arrangements to be back after lunch. The two men pulled away from the grocery as the sun was peeking over the trees. Dr. Grey didn't say much as they drove which was fine with Jack. His thoughts were taken up with the trinket he wanted to find for Meg. It had to be perfect.

Dr. Grey dropped Jack off in front of a jewelry store and gave simple directions to another not far away.

Jack pushed the door open. A bell chimed above him.

A small man with a handlebar mustache and thick glasses stepped from behind a thick curtain at the back of the shop. "How may I help you?"

Jack felt like a schoolboy under the man's scrutiny. He forced himself to stand still and not fidget with his hat. He cleared his throat. "I'm looking for something to give my girl when I ask her to marry me," he managed.

The man looked him up and down. "We have a selection of rings here, if you prefer them. Necklaces are in the case next to you."

Jack swung his gaze to the glass box on his left. He caught himself gaping at the shiny stones. "I think I'd like a ring."

The man lifted trays of rings from the case before him. Jack crossed the room and bent to look at the trinkets. He enquired after the price of one of them and staggered backward when he heard it.

"That's...that's a little outside my means. Do you have anything cheaper?"

The man behind the counter glared at him and produced a tray that had been concealed below the display. The stones were so tiny Jack could barely make them out on their thin bands.

It was his turn to glare. "Now that's just insulting."

"My good sir, I must encourage you to live within your means. We cater to a certain...clientele here at this shop. If you see nothing that catches your fancy, I'll have to encourage you to look elsewhere."

Jack straightened to his full height and looked down at the little man. "I'd be happy to take my business, my *money*, elsewhere. Thank you very much." He spun on his heal and stalked out of the store.

Jack followed Dr. Grey's directions until he reached a small shop a couple streets over. An old man who could have been Santa Claus looked up from cleaning the glass case when the bell rang. His jolly eyes glinted with a smile, though Jack couldn't see his mouth to know if it reached that far.

"You'll be needing a ring for a girl," the man said. Without waiting for a response, he walked to a case and opened it. "If you want new rings, we have these here. Those two trays are, shall we say, reclaimed rings. Some of them are vintage. Look it over. Prices are marked." He left Jack and returned to polishing the glass.

Jack leaned close over the rings in the case. The new rings were still far above anything he could afford. But a certain "reclaimed" ring stood out. It reminded him of the ring his granddad had given to his dad to give to his mom. And the price was perfect.

"Find something you like?"

Jack jumped back, startled, then burst out laughing. "I didn't see you there," he said.

"Sorry about that. Didn't mean to startle you. Are you interested in any of these?"

Jack pointed to the ring.

The old man beamed at him. "Good choice. I'll give you a discount since it strikes me that you're a soldier. Fresh back from France are you?"

Again, he didn't wait for Jack's response. Instead, he grabbed a polishing cloth and set to work cleaning the ring before he tucked it in a box and handed it to Jack. Jack gave the man his money, then tucked the box away in his trouser pocket.

Jack found his way back to the hospital and waited for Dr. Grey in the front waiting room. He'd only been away for a couple months but it seemed different, less hectic than before.

Dr. Grey wasn't surprised to see him. He shrugged into his coat and plunked his hat on his head. Jack followed him out to his car.

"Find what you were looking for?" Dr. Grey asked once they were on their way.

Jack grinned at him. He pulled the box out, opened it, and showed the ring to the doctor.

Dr. Grey let out a low whistle. "You were able to get that? They must have paid you pretty good in the army."

"Nah, it wasn't that. The ring is an antique. Vintage, I think the jeweler said. He gave me a discount, too. Think she'll like it?"

"Like it? She'll love it! But I promise not to breathe a word."

Chapter Thirty-two

Meg hadn't seen Nellie since her visit after the Ladies Aid ball. One afternoon, she decided to visit her. She walked over to Uncle Daniel and Aunt Elaine's house and knocked on the door. She waited for several minutes. The auto was parked in the garage. When neither Aunt Elaine or Nellie answered, she returned home, still wondering if she'd ever be on speaking terms with Nellie again.

About a week later, a letter arrived from Aunt Elaine in Boston, sharing that they decided to join Uncle Daniel. Nellie needed a change of scenery and Uncle Daniel had taken a teaching position for the semester. She was sorry they had left so abruptly, without saying goodbye, but she missed her husband and made the decision rather suddenly.

The month of March passed and ushered in April like a lamb. Unseasonably warm weather caused the snow to melt and early spring flowers to burst from the ground, celebrating the new season in all their boisterous color. Trees shyly put on soft green leaves, then grew bolder as the leaves darkened into deeper color.

The weather stayed warm enough that Gran insisted on putting in the garden. Meg knew there would be another cold snap. Gran knew this, too. The call of the warm outdoors was too much to resist.

They'd planted a garden in their plot for so many years that preparing the soil was simple. Gran got out the seeds and they laid out their garden plot. Then they started putting the seeds in the ground in neat rows. Jack came over after work and helped. Gran made iced tea. They all sat in the gathering dusk of evening and sipped their tea.

"This warm weather reminds me of when I was young. Your granddad would sit there and say 'We need to make our first trip to the beach!' We'd plan and prepare our picnic food. Most times, a doozy of a blizzard would blow up before we had a chance to get out there. Then we'd be forced to have our picnic in the living room in front of the fire." Gran chuckled at the memory. "Sometimes we'd get to go out to the beach in the good weather. We'd all come back with our first sunburn of the spring." She swiveled toward Meg. "You should take Jack to the beach. It's the last thing he needs to experience while he's here."

"I'd love that," Jack said. "I've been wanting to go ever since you told me about it. How far is it? How do we get there?"

"It's three miles out from town. We usually ride our bikes. Do you think you could ride a bike?" Meg wondered if Jack's stiff joints and scar tissue would allow him to pedal.

"I can try. Three miles isn't too far to walk, though. Shall we go tomorrow? Mr. Miller has given me the day off work."

"All I can say is you better get while the getting is good. This weather won't hold forever," Gran said. She pushed herself out of her chair and walked into the house.

"We have an extra bicycle you can try," Meg said.

They returned the gardening tools to the small shed and checked to see how the bicycles had fared the winter. Jack mounted the one bike with air still in the tires. Then, balancing on one leg, he placed his foot on the pedal and pushed off across the grass in the back yard.

"Haha! Look here! I'm doing it!" he called out in excitement. Gran stepped out the back door to watch him circle one of the apple trees and come back to the shed. He dropped the bike to the ground and stepped away from it. Meg and Gran cheered and clapped for his accomplishment. Meg shrieked and threw her arms around Jack's neck when he picked her up and swung her in a circle. He set her back on the ground, but didn't remove his arms. Meg heard the kitchen door shut. Gran had gone back inside the house.

Jack tightened his arms around her. "You push me to do things I would never try on my own," he said, serious. He lowered his lips to lightly brush hers. He pulled away, his gaze lingering on her mouth. Meg's breath caught. Jack's lips touched hers again, more urgent this time. His arms tightened around her as the kiss deepened. Meg melted into his kiss.

He was breathing hard when he finished. He rested his forehead against hers. A grin spread across his face. "Wow. That was even better than I'd imagined it would be."

Meg pulled away. She slid her hands down his arms and caught his hands. She gave him a shy smile. "Yes, it was."

"So. Tomorrow morning it is. I'll try to get here early enough to help with the food. This other bike might need some attention, too." Jack squeezed her fingers before releasing them.

"It sounds like a plan." Meg waved at Jack as he started home.

Meg almost expected to wake up to icy temperatures and snow on the ground. Instead, the brilliant sunshine held a promise that the afternoon would be quite hot. She knew it wouldn't last so she lifted her face to the bright sun and soaked it in, enjoying every bit of warmth. She intended to do the same with every moment of time with Jack today.

Jack arrived bright and early as he'd promised. He brought some fruit for their lunch. That, along with egg salad sandwiches, cookies, metal plates, and a picnic blanket, were tucked into a basket, which was tied onto one of the bikes. The other bike needed air in the tires and grease on the chain. Jack tested it on the road in front of the house and was convinced the tires would hold air. By mid-morning they were off on their adventure.

The trip took longer than normal. Jack tired easily. Sometimes he needed to stop and take a break or walk for a while. Meg didn't mind. She told him stories from her childhood. She pointed out the rocky hillside where her father and Uncle Daniel would take them climbing on their way to the beach. They'd climb high and look far out to sea.

Sometimes they could see fishing boats or ocean liners. Then they'd climb back down, hot and tired, ready to swim in the always-cold ocean.

They reached the beach. The path grew too sandy for the bikes. So they parked them by some rocks, untied the picnic basket, and set out with it across the sand. After a few feet of trying to manage shoes in the sand, Meg dropped onto the sandy path and peeled off her shoes and socks. She ran back and left those by the bikes. Jack watched the whole procedure, uncertainty written all over his face.

"I'm not sure if my feet will manage the sand very well," he said. "I'm afraid it will damage the scar tissue."

"I hadn't thought of that. Can you manage in your shoes? When we get to the picnic spot, you can take your shoes off and feel the sand between your toes if you want."

"That might work." Jack still didn't sound certain.

They struggled their way down the beach to what Meg insisted was the perfect spot. Three trees grew out of a grassy, rocky, protrusion into the sand of the beach. The spot would be shady all day long. They spread the blanket in the shade of the trees, sat on it and took in the view.

A stiff breeze blew steadily off the ocean. It cooled them from their bike ride and hike across the sand. Meg looked across the water, her knees drawn up and arms wrapped around them. The ocean was a deep teal blue, calm, except for a skim of foam on top of the waves that rolled in, one after the other. The splash of the waves onto the sand, the scrape as they went back out, the wind. They were hypnotized by it. Neither of them knew how much time had passed. Neither cared.

Meg shook herself out of her reverie and turned to Jack. "Are you hungry? Do you want lunch right now?"

Jack shook his head. "I have something I need to do, first." He took his shoes and socks off. Then he rolled his trouser legs up.

Meg cringed at the sight of the bloody lines criss-crossing his legs, where the scar tissue had broken and bled. They were covered with scabs from older wounds that hadn't quite healed. Jack had told her once that the scar tissue took longer to heal than skin would have. She could see this was true.

"Yeah, they are pretty ugly looking aren't they," Jack remarked ruefully as he struggled to his feet.

"It isn't that," Meg said."I didn't expect them to still be so red after all these months. Can you be more careful so the scar tissue doesn't break and bleed like that? Is it safe for you to be walking on the sand barefoot?"

"I have some salve that the doctor gave me that I use every day. He said they would eventually toughen up and wouldn't give me so much trouble. It might take several years, though. Hey! At least I still have legs, right? I'm one of the lucky ones." He winked at her, then grinned and held out his hand. She placed her hand in his and he pulled her to her feet. They walked to the water together.

"I can't go home without at least stepping into the ocean once," he said, standing as close to the water as he dared, without getting wet. The tide was coming in. Right then, a large wave broke on the sand where they were standing. Water splashed all over Jack's bare feet, up his legs and wet most of his trousers.

Jack yelled and jumped back with more speed than either of them thought possible. They both burst out laughing.

"Is it always that cold?" he gasped, as another wave wet the back of his retreating legs.

"Yep, pretty much all year," Meg replied through her own gasps. Her wet skirt clung to her legs. She gathered it in one hand to get it out of the way so she could move. "It gets a little warmer in the hottest part of the summer, but not much."

With a hoot of laughter, Jack spun around and ran into the water, up to his knees, then up to his waist. Then he plunged in all the way and swam out for a while. When he stood, the water was over his shoulders.

"Come on in!" he called, his teeth chattering. "The water's fine!"

"You are crazy!" Meg called back and laughed at him. But she waded out into the water. The wet sand and seaweed squished up between her toes.

Jack swam back most of the way, then stood and walked toward her. "You're right. Turns out the ocean isn't so bad after all. Now I can go home to my little country town and tell them I got to swim in it." He caught her hand in his own and skimmed his thumb over her knuckles. "Okay, we can eat lunch. I'll have enough time to dry before we head back." He tugged her up the beach to their blanket.

The tide came in, slowly, but surely. Their picnic spot was well above the dry line. The sun shone down, bright and hot for an early April day. Jack's clothes dried. He finished eating and stretched out on the blanket, content.

"I wish this didn't have to end," he said, his eyes closed.

Meg, hugging her knees again, silently agreed with him. The brisk breeze had loosened her hair from its pins. She tucked an annoying strand behind her ear where it would be less of a bother.

"Don't do that," Jack said. He rolled onto his side to observe her. "I've been lying here pretending it's my finger stroking your soft cheek and imagining what it would feel like if it was."

Meg flushed and dropped her gaze. The strand came loose on its own and brushed past her cheek.

"That's better." Jack rolled onto his back and tucked his hands behind his head. "You're quiet this afternoon. What's on your mind?"

"I was thinking we didn't have many days like this left before you have to go home. I want to hang on to every minute. It's kind of silly." She started to brush the hair back again.

Jack reached across and caught her hand. He intertwined his fingers with hers. "It isn't silly. I've been feeling the same way. When I leave, I want you to remember that I'm not going to be gone forever. I'll take care of things for my parents and then come back for you. I promise. Here, I have something to show you."

He sat up and produced a small black box from somewhere in the grasses next to the blanket. "I love you, Meg. I have from the first moment I met you. I want to spend the rest of my life with you. Will you marry me?"

Jack handed Meg the open box and she saw the ring he offered. She met his gaze. Her eyes filled with tears. A gust of wind blew the hair across her eyes. Jack caught it and tucked it behind her ear. His fingers slid into her hair and cradled the back of her head. He leaned toward her and claimed her lips with his own. Meg kissed him back. The tears slid, unhindered, down her cheeks. When he pulled away, he kissed them away one by one.

"Don't cry, darling. You're supposed to be happy."

Meg laughed through her tears. "I am happy. And sad. Yes, I'll marry you. But I miss you already."

Jack ran his thumb across her cheek and kissed her one more time. "I miss you, too." He slid the ring onto her finger. They both admired it as it sparkled in the sunlight.

The wind changed directions that moment. A cold gust blew across their place in the sun. Meg glanced up at the sky. She couldn't see any difference yet, but she knew they needed to start home. She sighed and squeezed Jack's hand, then released it and began packing up their lunch things. "We'd better go. A storm is on its way."

Jack felt the difference in the wind as well. He pulled on his socks and shoes. By the time he had finished, Meg had the lunch things put away. He stood up. She picked up the blanket and folded it. Jack picked up the basket. Then he took her hand again. They walked back up the beach in silence, neither wanting to say everything they were thinking.

When they reached the bicycles, it was Meg's turn to pull on her stockings and shoes. A cloud covered the sun. The sand lost its residual warmth. A gust of wind made her shiver.

Jack looked up at the sky. High, light clouds had covered the brilliant blue. The weather was changing, just as they expected. They tied the basket onto the bike, then clambered on and started home. Jack pushed himself harder on the return trip. He didn't want to get caught out in bad weather.

By the time they reached Gran's house, a light drizzle was falling. Meg hurried the picnic things off the bikes, then Jack put them back in the shed. Gran had a pot of soup heating on the stove. It smelled wonderful. When Gran invited him to stay for supper, Jack agreed.

Gran giggled like a schoolgirl when they told her their news and Meg showed her the ring. She hugged them and clapped them on the back. But Meg saw her sneak her handkerchief out of her pocket when she thought no one was watching.

Meg slipped up behind her and gave her a hug.

"I'm happy for you, dearie. I've known this day was coming for a long time. These are happy tears for you and that boy over there."

"Thanks, Gran," Meg whispered and kissed Gran's cheek.

By the time they finished supper and Jack was preparing to leave it was pouring outside. The weather matched Meg's mood. Jack waited on the porch until she brought him a slicker.

"Thank you for a lovely day," she said, smiling up at him, though tears threatened every moment.

Jack pulled the slicker over his head and looked down at her for a moment, as though he was trying to commit every detail to memory. Then he cupped her face with his hands, stroking her cheek with his thumb, like he had at the beach.

"I had a wonderful time, myself. Thank you for taking me." He kissed her on the cheek, then disappeared into the darkness, pulling up the hood of the slicker as he walked down the porch stairs.

Meg watched his dim figure walk up the street. She thought she saw him look back and wave before he turned toward the grocery. Then he was gone. Meg stumbled into the house and up the stairs to her room. She threw herself onto her bed and sobbed. He wasn't leaving for another week or two, but it felt like they had said goodbye today. In the morning, everything would feel better, but not tonight.

Chapter Thirty-three

Meg woke in the middle of the night. She was stretched across her bed, fully dressed and freezing cold. She stumbled around in the pitch black, pulled off her salt-stiff clothes, and pulled on her warm nightgown. Then she burrowed under the covers on her bed. When she woke again in the gray morning, a thick blanket of snow covered the ground once more.

Meg struggled out of bed and into clean clothes. She could hear Gran banging around in the kitchen. Life continued as normal. She thought back to the morning after her mother had died. Dad had died a week earlier, but mother had been so sick at the time that Meg had barely had time to attend the funeral before she was back at the hospital with her mother. But when mother was dead, it felt as though there was nothing left. The future stretched before her, bleak, uncertain.

Meg felt the same this morning even though this wasn't anything like that. She sank onto the bed and tried to talk herself out of her despondency. Jack was going away for a few months. Meg could write him letters. He'd reply when he had time. She gazed at the ring on her finger and knew she would see him again. They *would* be apart, but the time would go by quickly. She had nothing to cry about.

Meg combed her hair and pinned it up in a coil at the nape of her neck. She put the brush back on the dresser, squared her shoulders and lifted her chin. She smiled at her reflection. *I'm getting married to Jack*, she thought. Her brown eyes sparkled back at her, filled with happiness at the thought though she could see the sadness lingering in the background.

Meg entered the kitchen a few minutes later to find several rows of small pots along the wall. She gave Gran a puzzled look.

Gran didn't even glance up from the oatmeal she was stirring on the stove.

"I thought I should bring those in from the shed since it is below freezing. We'll have to wait and see what happens to the seeds we planted in the garden. I'm always too eager to start." Gran sighed and shook her head.

"You went outside this morning in the snow to bring those inside?" Meg asked.

"I brought them in last night before it got too cold. I was afraid if I waited until this morning it would be too late. They've only been planted for a couple days so they might be okay. I hated to take a chance." Gran said.

"I should have helped you. I had no idea you were doing it. Jack probably would have stayed and helped, too."

"You both had a busy day and were tired. Besides, it only took me a few minutes. Then I went to bed, too. I slept in this morning because of weather." Gran smiled and set two bowls of the lumpy, white mush on the table. "Let's sit up and eat it while it's good and hot."

Meg was thankful for the quiet day at home. The snow fell steadily all morning. By early afternoon, it had tapered off, then stopped. This wet snow wouldn't work well for sledding. However, the snow was perfect for building a snowman. When Meg heard the Stuart girls shrieking with laughter outside, she got into her warm things and joined them.

The sun came out and shone on them while they built a huge snowman from the snow in both their front yards. They found sticks for arms and rocks for buttons, a mouth, and eyes. An old rag made a perfect scarf. The Stuart girls insisted that a carrot must be used for a nose. Gran didn't have one. Neither did the Stuarts. So they gave up found a oddly shaped stick instead.

After another cold night, the weather warmed, little by little. The snow melted off. The temperature became more seasonal.

Jack came over in time to see the snowman before it fell down.

"You okay?" he asked the first minute he could get alone with Meg.

"Yes. I'm alright. I was being silly the other day." She smiled at him.

"You weren't being silly. I knew how you felt," he said.

"I *was* being silly," Meg insisted. "I was acting as though you were leaving forever. But we're only going to be apart for a few months. Those will go by before we even know it.

"When I woke up the next morning, I realized I was allowing myself to feel like I did after my parents died – hopeless, without direction, distraught. The truth is, I have no reason to feel that way. I was being silly."

"I want you to miss me. I mean, if you go on as usual, what difference have I made?"

"I'll miss you. Count on it," Meg assured him. "Do you know when you're leaving?"

"That is one reason I came over tonight," Jack said. "Dr. Grey cleared me for travel anytime. I felt like I needed to give Mr. Miller a chance to find a replacement, so I thought maybe I'd try to get a train ticket for a week from Friday."

The time was shorter than Meg had hoped it would be.

"So soon? That doesn't leave much time."

"I know." Jack laid his hand on her forearm and squeezed it. Then he sighed. "I can't promise to write letters to you. I'm terrible at that. If I made that promise and then failed to deliver, I'd hate myself. I'll promise to try, though. Is that good enough for you?"

The concern in his voice made Meg smile at him. She covered his hand with her own and squeezed it. "It's great with me. You know

I'll appreciate anything I get. That said, I *do* promise to write you. As often as I can, in fact."

"Good." Jack grinned at her. "I'll look forward to it."

Chapter Thirty-four

The day of Jack's departure dawned bright and sunny. His train didn't leave until late afternoon. He planned to spend the whole day with them. Jack had come over for supper every night that week. They played checkers late into the evening, until he reluctantly left.

The day of his departure, he didn't arrive at their house until almost noon. He had cleaned the small apartment behind the grocery that had been his home for the last few months. All his belongings fit into a carpet bag and small suitcase, which he set in the hall, by the front door.

"This feels so strange," he commented as he rubbed his hands on his trouser legs. "Everything feels so normal, when, in reality, I'm leaving in a few hours." He hesitated. "There is still time to change my mind, you know."

"You need to go back. Your father needs you." Meg smiled up at him. "Come on. Gran is fixing lunch. She might let you have some of those snickerdoodles we baked last night if you promise not to let it ruin your lunch."

Jack grinned. "As if that could ever happen." He followed Meg down the hall to the kitchen.

The rows of pots in the kitchen had small sprouts poking out of the soil. Meg and Gran had carried them back out to the shed one morning, only to have to bring them in again ahead of a freeze that night. The kitchen had been their home ever since.

Jack stepped around some of the pots and took a seat at the small table which was already set for lunch. He heaved a relieved sigh. "I am amazed how dirty a room can get after only a few months of living there, even though I've cleaned it every week." He shook is head. "I couldn't believe the dust I found.

"Then, Dr. Grey picked up my ticket from the station in Walton. When I got it from him, I discovered I'd told my parents the wrong train in my last letter. So I had to send a telegram this morning to be sure they'd have the right one." Jack rested his head against the wall behind him and closed his eyes. "It's been a long morning."

Gran pulled the steaming meat pie out of the oven and set it on the table in front of them. She placed a pan of sweet potatoes on the table, then a dish of green beans.

"Eat up, sonny," she said, patting him on the shoulder. "I wanted you to get at least one good meal tucked away to keep you until you got home. We'll pack some lunch things for you to eat on the trip." Gran walked around the table and took her normal seat, while Meg pulled up the kitchen stool and sat on it.

"I'm having a hard time getting used to the thought that I'm really going home," Jack said as they ate. "I've been gone for almost three years. So many times, in those foxholes, I thought I was a goner for sure. Here I am, older, hopefully wiser, headed back to the farm. And I'm nervous. There is no logical explanation for feeling nervous."

"You've changed. They've changed. It's a lot to deal with all at once," Gran remarked. "I'd be nervous, too."

"I hadn't thought of the fact that they've changed. You're right. We might have some adjustments to make when I get back. I wasn't much more than a kid when I left. I could put in a hard day's work with the best of them. But I've seen so many horrible things. The last three years have changed me. I hope it's been for the better."

"I'm sure your Dad will be pleased with the man who comes home on the train tomorrow." Gran reached across the small table and patted Jack's hand with a smile.

Dr. Grey arrived to take Jack to the station in Walton long before any of them were ready for him to leave. Meg felt like her stomach sank all the way into her shoes when she heard his car drive up to their house. A lump formed in her throat. She tried to swallow and talk around it, but couldn't seem to manage. Jack didn't say anything, either. He stood and walked into the hallway. Picking up his luggage, he stepped outside and carried it down to Dr. Grey's car. They spoke for a moment or two. Then Jack came back to the house.

"It's time," he stated, looking from Gran to Meg with an expression that Meg had never seen on his face before. He walked across the room and engulfed Gran in a bear hug, holding her tightly without saying a word. When he let her go, tears were streaming down the elderly woman's face.

"I love you, you dear boy," she said through the tears, taking his face in her hands. She pulled his face down and gave him a firm kiss on the cheek. "You go out there and make me proud, just like you have with everything else you've done here. You'll be back before you know it." Gran stepped away and hurried out of the room, with the excuse of needing to find a handkerchief.

Jack fidgeted with his hat, and regarded Meg. "If your Gran doesn't mind, I asked Dr. Grey if you could come along. He said he'd have you home by early evening."

Meg's heart lifted. All they were doing was prolonging the inevitable, something she was preferring to do more and more as the time of his departure came closer.

Meg found Gran in the kitchen, sniffing and blowing her nose, banging pots and pans around with the pretense of trying to find the right one to make soup. Gran stopped long enough to hear that Meg was going with Jack to the station, then turned back to her clanging and banging.

They rode in relative silence. Dr. Grey chatted with Jack. Meg made the occasional comment. When they arrived at the station, Dr. Grey helped Jack unload his bags and then told them he'd wait at the car.

The departing train was waiting to leave. A few people meandered up and down the platform. A woman was saying goodbye to a young couple with a tiny baby. Two soldiers in uniform laughed and joked about something with a third man who appeared to be the one leaving.

Jack walked toward a car and showed his ticket to the porter who pointed directions. Jack walked over to the stairs leading into it and set his bags at the edge of the platform. Meg followed. He turned to face her.

"I guess this is finally it," he said. "We've put it off as long as possible." He reached down and took both of her hands into his own and held them. "I'm going to miss you. Take care of yourself and Gran."

Meg smiled up at him. "I'm going to miss you, too. Try not to overdo it at first."

"People told me I was one of the lucky ones. I'd lived through the war, through the flu. My legs were burned but I could learn to use them again. I didn't believe them. I hated them for saying it. Then you walked in my room that I day and everything changed. You made me feel like one of the lucky ones. You made me feel like trying when I didn't want to. So, yeah. I'll take it easy on myself at first. But every time I walk anywhere, I'll be reminded of a brown-haired girl — my girl — who made it possible."

Meg squeezed Jack's fingers. She couldn't stop the tears that slid down her cheeks and dripped off her chin. "I like it when you call me your girl."

Jack brushed the tears away with the back of his hand. "I love you."

"I love you, too," Meg whispered.

The conductor swung out of the first car. "All aboard!"

Everyone on the platform moved toward their respective cars. Jack released her hand. "I'm not going to say it. This isn't 'goodbye'. We'll be together before you know it. I'm going to write you." He turned, picked up his bags, and stepped onto the train. Then he stopped.

He dropped his bags where they had been before and turned back to Meg. He wrapped his arms around her. His lips met hers with longing, desire, passion.

For a moment, it seemed to Meg like time stopped. She put her arms around his neck and kissed him back, holding him like she would never let go.

The second cry of "All aboard" brought both of them back to reality. Jack pulled away. His hands slid from her her back, down her arms. He squeezed both her hands with his own one more time. Without a word he turned and, picking up his luggage, boarded the train.

Meg didn't move. She watched as he found a seat and secured his bags in the overhead rack. The train lurched forward. Jack opened his window and leaned out, waving with all his might as they pulled away.

Meg watched and waved until the train was completely out of sight.

He was gone.

Chapter Thirty-five

April 21

Dear Jack,

The last few days since you've been gone have been eventful. The day after you left the apple trees began blossoming. They are loaded with buds. Gran is worried the cool nights we've been having will damage them. I think the blossoms look good and she needn't worry. The harvest in a few months is promising to be a good one. We'll have our hands full making all the preserves and apple butter, and jelly. It wouldn't be fall without all that work, though I enjoy it and dread it at the same time.

The plants in the garden are poking their little green heads up out of the ground. We've had to weed it the last few days. Why are the weeds hardier and come up faster than the plants? Gran is eager to get the plants we're keeping in the kitchen into the ground.

Uncle Daniel and Aunt Elaine came back a couple days ago! They visited us yesterday. Nellie decided to stay in Boston for a while with Uncle Daniel's sister. Aunt Elaine said that she didn't want any letters yet. She said Nellie was doing well and getting over what had happened here. Gran told me after they left that she thinks Nellie is being dramatic about it all, as usual. I don't know what to think about it. It hurts that she is acting like I was involved somehow. They'll return to Boston by the end of the week so Uncle Daniel can finish his term at the university.

May 5

Dear Meg,

I arrived back safely and without event. Everyone in town made a big fuss. They had a parade and gave me a plaque.

Thankfully, since then things have settled down. I guess you could call it settled down. I've barely had a minute to sit down to do anything, even eat. I think we've pretty much got it all planted, though. I hope we aren't too late getting it in. Mom needed help getting her garden in, too. I got to plant two gardens this year. Helping her made me think of you.

I've been thinking about you a lot. I see things every day that you would enjoy, or that I'd like to tell you about. I miss you.

Well, Mom just came in to tell me that she's ready right now to leave for town. She's mailing this for me. It's a lot shorter than I wanted it to be, but I guess it will have to do for now.

May 15,

Dear Jack,

I'm so glad you made it back safely! Gran kept saying no news was good news. I couldn't help but worry a little. I'm glad that they welcomed you back so well. A brave, hometown soldier returned from the war. You deserved it!

I had a letter from Nellie yesterday! She says she has a beau! "Real live and truly for real" were her exact words. I feel guilty for being so skeptical, but seeing will be believing with this one.

The church picnic was last Saturday. It was great fun. We baked all day Friday for it. Gran made her famous apple crumb cake. We took a big roast with all the fixings. The games after the meal were so much fun! Emily Stuart and I were in a three leg race together. It's been a very long time since I laughed that hard. We thought we had it worked out to start together but, in her excitement, Emily put the wrong foot forward first. We managed to catch ourselves before falling, but got out of step again and tumbled. Even with our slow start we still weren't the last team. Several pairs of smaller people were behind us. They tripped and fell. Other teams couldn't get

191

around the fallen racers and they tripped, too. We had a pile of people in the middle of the field. Teams tried to dodge around it, but only managed to fall in a different spot. It was like watching dominoes fall. The pair in front fell when they looked back to find out what all the commotion was about. Reverend Norton finally just called the race and we started over. Not one single team finished the first time.

Mr. Miller got a new stock boy. His nephew has come to live with them. I'm not sure of all the details, but I think the parents died in the epidemic last fall and they've divided up their six children among relatives. I feel so bad for them. Nothing like adding insult to injury. First you lose your parents, then you get farmed out all over the countryside. It isn't fair.

May 23,

Dear Jack,

The rest of the garden is finally planted. It's been in for a couple days now. The plants that were out there already look fine, even after those cold nights that we had late in the season.

The weather is warming up, too. We might have to cut our grass in a few days because it is growing so well. I love this time of year. The flowers in the beds are coming up and look good. The tulips are almost finished for the season. I think they are finishing late, but Gran insists it's normal. The peonies are starting to put on buds. The roses are beginning to think about forming buds as well. I'm looking forward to those the most. My father planted the two biggest rose bushes in the flower beds for his mother on her birthday. I love them. They grow the most beautiful pink and deep red roses you've ever seen.

Aunt Elaine came over the other day. She said that Nellie was planning to come for a visit and bring her beau. I guess he's real if they are talking about him, too. She also told me she would like to go back to volunteer at the hospital now and then, and asked if I would join her. Gran thinks I should. She says I shouldn't be cooped up in the house so much. I guess I'll do it.

June 15,

Dear Jack,

Nellie and her beau, Edward, visited just as they promised. Nellie is, well, Nellie. She doesn't seem to have changed much. The bright side of all this is that Edward doesn't seem to mind her. He seems to like being around her. Her incessant talking doesn't put him off, either. He's a quiet man. She said he's a bank clerk, but is related to the man in charge of the bank so has a lot of room for advancement in his job. I guess that matters a lot to Nellie. She's told everyone.

Truth is, I'm kind of annoyed with the whole situation. Aunt Elaine said that Edward would like them to get married in a year or two, so he'd have time to work his way up in the bank and earn more money than he does now. Nellie is pushing to marry right away. She says she doesn't mind being poor, but we all know better. I feel the worst for Edward.

Not that any of this is my business. Thanks for letting me tell you about it. I know you can't do anything about it because you are so far away.

On a lighter note, Aunt Elaine and I have been going to the hospital once a week. I'm so happy to be able to see people there again! So far, I've been helping with the children. I was surprised to be allowed to do that. I figured they'd put me back at the mending or cooking.

When Nellie was here, we all went out to the ocean. Even Gran went along because Uncle Daniel was driving. We didn't walk all the way to the trees where you and I sat. Gran couldn't make it all the way there and back again without help. Walking in the sand is too difficult for her. So we sat at the picnic tables close to where you and I parked our bicycles. I didn't do any swimming this time, either. The water was too cold!

July 1,

Dear Jack,

It's official. Nellie and Edward are engaged. That part wasn't the most surprising, however. The most surprising was that they plan to marry in September. On top of that, she wants to marry in Boston. Gran and I won't be going. Gran couldn't make that trip.

Uncle Daniel isn't very happy about the whole thing. His sister is the one helping Nellie with everything. I think Aunt Elaine is hurt that Nellie didn't want her help to plan the wedding. I don't blame her. Uncle Daniel and Aunt Elaine came over and talked it all over with Gran. Gran told me later she thinks Uncle Daniel should put his foot down and make her wait the two years Edward thinks would be wise. Personally, I think she wants to be married before I am, even though we haven't set a date.

The weather turned hot a week or so ago. We haven't had a lot of rain. Gran has been watering in the garden. Why is it that even when there isn't enough rain to make the plants grow properly, the weeds still grow like crazy? We've been getting out to do the weeding in the garden and flower beds early in the morning. Even then, we're drenched with sweat before we're done.

July 5,

Dear Jack,

Uncle Daniel and Aunt Elaine went up to Boston after their talk with Gran the other day. We haven't heard anything yet. I'll keep you posted.

We celebrated Independence Day with the Stuarts. They had a big fair in Hollis. We all walked up together. The mayor gave a speech. So did Dr. Grey. You would have been proud. One of the boys recited the Gettysburg Address and some other children took turns quoting from the Constitution. They had a band and pony rides. Someone even brought ice cream. Gran tired herself out, but I think she enjoyed every minute. They set off fireworks after dark. That was the best part of all. The band played the whole time, though you could barely hear the music over the loud explosions.

194

Today was the hottest day yet. The Stuart girls and I walked out to the ocean and went swimming. It felt heavenly! The water is still icy cold, but the sand was so hot that our feet needed the relief of the water by the time they reached it. We jumped in and splashed and played for a long time. The younger girls brought buckets and little trowels and we built a wall in the wet sand. When the tide began to come in again, we pretended it was a moat surrounding a castle. So we built up a sort of sand castle in the middle. It didn't last long, though. The water washed it right away.

I have a sunburn and am tired from the last two days. But it was worth every bit of it.

July 12,

Dear Meg,

I know I didn't promise to write. Even so, I intended to write as often as possible. Apparently, that wasn't very often. I love your letters. They help me feel a part of things there.

We're taking a break from some of the work tonight. I have to. We've been having a heat spell, too. I've been pushing myself too hard with the farm work and getting dizzy spells. Dad brought us in early from the field today. We'll do our evening chores in a few minutes but we all needed to get in out of the heat for while this afternoon.

Mom goes out and waters her garden every morning and night, but the poor little plants still look wilted by mid-afternoon. However, we're getting a bumper crop of the best tasting watermelons I've ever had. Maybe they taste better because I haven't had any for three years. I don't know. It's like eating candy. Mom is getting a lot of cucumbers, too. She's putting most of them up in pickles – that is, all the ones she rescues from Steve and Dad and me.

Our Independence Day sounds a lot like yours. We took the day off and spent it in town at the big town picnic they were having. Steve raced one of our horses and won. We all ate way too much. They had this big tank full of water with a seat suspended over it. Someone sat on the seat and another person threw a ball at a target. If the ball hit

195

the target the guy on seat would get dunked into the tank. Dad talked me into getting up there. Wouldn't you know, Steve is a dead eye with a baseball. One pitch and I was soaking wet in that tank. I'd never admit this to Steve, but it felt pretty good to cool down in that water. In the afternoon, we had a baseball game – town folk versus country folk. We country folk creamed those town boys.

I hope things work out with Nellie and Edward.

We never talked about how or where we'd get married. I'd love to hear what kind of wedding you want. I don't know when I'll be able to get away and come for you, though. Every day I think "Tomorrow, I'll just up and leave and go marry her and bring her here." But the next day I wake up and get started with my work and the day is finished before I have a chance to leave.

I miss you so much.

July 30,

Dear Jack,

The worst of the heat finally broke a few days ago in some terrible storms. We had to go down to the root cellar for one of them. Imagine, if you will, Gran sitting on last years potatoes knitting by lamplight while the storm raged above. Thankfully, it was over quickly and then rained the rest of the night and all the next day. The weather is much more like normal for this time of year. It's still hot, but not as oppressive.

I've been thinking a lot about our wedding. I've always wanted a quiet wedding at church with family and a few friends. However, I'm not sure how that would work for us. You live there with all your family. All I have is Gran, Uncle Daniel and Aunt Elaine. You have more family than I do. On the other hand, if we tried to have it there, Gran would most certainly not be able to come. So I'm torn. It would be wonderful to have your family at the wedding, but I want Gran at my wedding.

Gran and I talked about this the other day. She thinks we should be married here in a small wedding and have a reception out there. I hate to make plans for your side of the family, but her idea does seem the easiest for everyone.

A few days ago, when Aunt Elaine and I were in Walton at the hospital, we met Mrs. Fulton, Dr. Fulton's wife. She heard you and I were engaged and she said she had some fabric she wanted me to see. So we went to her house after we finished at the hospital. She gave me the most beautiful dark brown wool suiting you've ever seen. It is so smooth and drapes beautifully! She said it could be a going away outfit, but I was thinking it would make a nice wedding suit. Gran and I have been deciding on a pattern for it.

August 7,

Dear Jack,

Uncle Daniel and Aunt Elaine are back with Nellie. Uncle Daniel put his foot down and insisted that she and Edward wait to get married until Edward is ready for it. Nellie is not happy with them. I still haven't seen her. It hurts that she wants nothing to do with me. I've tried to apologize, though I can't even imagine what I did to her. Gran says the only mistake I made was to be right

We've been canning tomatoes like crazy the last few days. The green beans are still growing. I have to pick them every day. There are two huge pumpkins in the garden that will be ready for this fall, along with quite a few smaller ones.

Gran cut out my wedding suit a couple days ago and we started sewing it. I'm so excited about it! Suddenly, with this occurrence, the whole thing seems real.

August 15,

Dear Meg,

We've got the corn harvested and we're getting ready to start mowing hay. Tonight, we finished a little earlier than normal so I had some breathing time. Thought I better send you a note so you'd know for sure I was still alive.

I talked with Mom and Dad about the wedding. They said they'd be glad to travel out there for a small wedding if it meant your Gran could come. They can have a thing here afterward for the rest of my family. I couldn't live with myself if your Gran wasn't able to come to your wedding.

A couple things happened this last week. The first was that I traveled to my friend Cavanaugh's hometown to see his widow and daughter. I promised him I'd do it almost a year ago. It took me a couple hours to get there by train and then I walked to the address I had from him. His wife didn't live at that house anymore. The people who were there said she'd moved to live with her mom and gave me direction.

It's one of the hardest things I've ever done, Meg. I saw that woman from the picture and the baby who's now a toddler swinging on their porch swing and broke down and cried. Why did Cavanaugh have to die?

Once I'd gotten myself together, I went up to the house and told them who I was. I gave them back the picture with his dried blood on it and gave her his message in person. She bolted up off that swing and disappeared into the house, leaving me with the baby. The baby didn't mind me as long as I kept the swing going. She even climbed onto my lap and played with the clasps on my overalls. Her mom and grandma came out after a while. We talked until I had to get back to the station to catch the train for home.

I still have nightmares about that night in the trenches last year. I hear the artillery exploding in the distance and feel Cavanaugh's blood pooling under us, warm and sticky. I hear his words, "Tell her I love her." That could have been me, Meg. It should have been me. Then I'd never have met you. Your life would be taking a different path than it has.

Everything that happened that night in France brought me to the point of meeting you. I never want to experience the pain or suffering again, but I've come to the point where I'm thankful for it, because it brought you into my life.

But, enough of that.

The other thing that happened is supposed to be a surprise. I don't know how long I can keep it. I'm terrible at keeping secrets. I'm going to give you a hint. Let's just say I found a way to spend what I earned as a soldier. Mom saved everything I had sent back to them and it turned into a little nest egg. That's all I'm telling until I see you next. Well, hopefully, anyway. I'm going to try my best to keep this secret.

August 28,

Dear Jack,

My suit is ready. I talked with Reverend Norton about marrying us. He said we could use the church for it any time. I talked with Dr. Grey, Nurse Rogers, and Dr. and Mrs. Fulton, too. They said they'd all be ready to attend whenever you arrived.

Nellie still won't speak to me. I wanted her to stand up with me, but when I've gone over there she stays in her room. It's hurtful, but there is nothing I can do about it.

I can hardly wait to find out what your secret is! Most of all, when you tell me your secret, it means you will be here and we'll be together. Forever.

Chapter Thirty-six

September, 1919

The apples were ready to be picked. Gran had been checking every day for a week to see if it was time. Now and then the ripe ones would fall onto the ground. They would hurry to get them before the birds or bugs made them inedible.

As Meg walked home from church that Sunday afternoon, she thought back to a year before when similar events had taken place. So many things had changed in the past year.

Gran could no longer walk to church. Most Sundays, Uncle Daniel picked her up and took her. Today, however, they were away visiting Boston, so Meg had walked on her own while Gran stayed home. Meg took careful notes of the sermon so she could tell Gran every detail.

Last year, Nellie came over to help with the apple picking. This year, she was barely speaking to her parents, let alone Meg and Gran. Meg hadn't seen her in months. Even when Meg went to visit Aunt Elaine or take things over there from Gran, Nellie stayed in her room.

Last year, Meg had yet to meet Jack. Now they were engaged and she was waiting for him to come for her. The brown suit hung in the hall closet, draped in an old sheet to keep the dust off. Waiting. Meg felt as if she was going to have to wait forever. The summer had seemed so long. Jack's letters had been sweet, but there hadn't been many of them.

The house was silent when Meg entered. Gran must be napping. Meg was worried about her, but Uncle Daniel insisted nothing was wrong. It was not normal for Gran to sit idle so often in the afternoon. Nor was it normal for her to require a nap in both the morning and afternoon. She struggled to walk from the front of the house to the back. Meg wasn't sure when it had begun. She'd never recovered her full strength after she had pneumonia last fall. She was spunky and had hidden it well. She'd been gradually failing and no one had realized how much until now.

Meg crept from the front door, through the hallway to the kitchen. As she passed the living room she could see Gran sleeping on the couch. A few things were set out in the kitchen for lunch. Meg had started some soup the evening before. This sat in a large pot on the stove. Very little was needed for it to be finished so Meg tied on an apron and began to work as quietly as possible. Uncle Daniel would need to come again to check on Gran when he arrived back this week. Meg would insist on it.

Monday morning dawned sunny and crisp. The weather was perfect for picking apples. Meg started as soon as breakfast was finished and the dishes washed, planning to work all day. Gran came out and sat on the back stoop, watching. At first, she would walk out to the trees to take the full baskets from Meg and give her empty ones. By noon, even that was too much.

That evening, Meg knew she needed more help. She walked next door to talk to Mrs. Stuart. A cacophony of girlish voices could be heard through the front door as Meg knocked. Little Penny answered it and, instead of inviting Meg inside, ran back to the rest of the girls to announce her arrival. Meg stepped through the door and was met by Mrs. Stuart.

"How are you?" the lady greeted. "How is your Gran? Is she doing any better?"

Meg shook her head. "No. I wish she was. I picked apples today. She tried to help, but it was too much for her. That's why I came over. I know the older girls are in school, but I was wondering if you and

Penny can come and help. There won't be much in the way of pay, unless you count taking all the apples you want when we're finished."

"Penny and I would love to be able to do that," said Mrs. Stuart, excited. "She begged me all day today to go out and help you. She was so disappointed when I wouldn't let her. We'll plan to help every day until the job is done. The older girls can help when they get home from school."

Meg sighed with relief and grinned at the lady before her. "You can not imagine how thankful I am you can help. Well then, I guess I'll see you in the morning."

They finished picking the apples that week. The Stuarts took several large buckets of them to their house. Meg began the work to get the ones they kept made into all the delicious things Gran loved.

On Monday of the following week, Gran couldn't get out of bed. Meg hurried to get Uncle Daniel, only to discover they still hadn't returned from Boston. So she brought Dr. Grey instead.

"It's her heart," he said gravely as he shrugged back into his black overcoat on the way out of the house. "There isn't much I can do for her. She needs to rest if she feels like it. However, try to encourage her to get out of bed and walk about the house. I've given her something for the pain so she might sleep for a little while."

"She's in pain?" Meg gasped in surprise and horror. "She never said anything. Uncle Daniel has been here over and over again because I was so worried about her. She never said anything at all about it." Tears sprang to her eyes.

"She told me she didn't want to worry Daniel or you. She thought the pain was nothing." Dr. Grey patted Meg's shoulder. "Your grandmother is a strong woman. She won't go without a fight. She wants to see you married to that young man of yours. I'll be back to check on her tomorrow." Then he put his hat on and hurried out the door and down the walk.

Gran was sleeping when Meg checked on her. She closed the door and went into the kitchen. Piles of apples covered the counter and table in the kitchen. More bubbled on the stove in various stages of preparation. Meg looked around the room, a familiar grief filling her heart as she did it. She half-heartedly stirred the pots on the stove then moved to peel more apples at the counter.

A sob caught in her throat and tears filled her eyes. This kitchen work had always been Gran's favorite part of the apple harvest. This year, Meg was left to do it herself because Gran was far worse off than any of them realized. She couldn't take any more. She removed the boiling pots from the stove.

Meg hurried from the kitchen. Grabbing a sweater on her way past the pegs by the front door, she slipped outside.

The weather had turned cold, unseasonable for the end of September. Meg pulled the sweater on and walked, not paying attention to where she was going, thinking. She felt like her world was falling in around her. Gran was dying. In the last months, she'd often wondered what Gran would do without her there to help. Now she didn't have to wonder.

Tears came and flowed down her cheeks as she walked, obscuring her vision. What if Gran didn't even make it until Jack returned and she could see them married? How would she deal with losing Gran? She'd been there for Meg when Meg's parents had died. She'd loved her, cared for her, listened to her, encouraged her. The agony of the impending loss overwhelmed Meg. She sank onto a bench in the town park and sobbed.

The tears spent, Meg gathered her composure and stood up. She needed to get home.

The gray sky matched her mood for the afternoon. It also made it feel much later and darker than it was. Meg hurried to get back before Emily Stuart arrived after school to help with the apples. As she approached the house, she noticed a man sitting on the porch swing, rocking it back and forth. She was still too far away to tell who it was. It had to be Uncle Daniel. Maybe she should insist he talk with Dr. Grey.

She drew closer to the house. It wasn't Uncle Daniel. The man was taller, thinner, and wore a flat cap, instead of Uncle Daniel's familiar fedora. He stood from the swing as she came closer.

Stepping out of the shadows of the porch, Meg could finally see his face.

Jack.

A sob caught in Meg's throat once again. She stumbled forward, running.

Jack didn't say anything. He met her at the beginning of the walk and caught her in his arms. His strong arms. Meg caught the fabric of his jacket, buried her face in it, and sobbed once more, this time with relief and happiness.

"Are you alright?" Jack asked with concern when she'd calmed down.

Meg pulled away with a half sob, half laugh. "Yes! You're here! When did you arrive? How did you get here?"

"I only just arrived a few minutes ago. I wanted to surprise you so I asked Dr. Grey to fetch me from the station. He was more than happy to do it, too. He wouldn't tell me what was going on, but he said I couldn't have come at a better time."

"Come inside! We shouldn't be standing out here in the cold talking. Besides, Gran might be awake and she'll be so happy to see you!" Meg was laughing now, wiping her eyes. She pulled away from him and turned toward the house.

Jack kept hold of her hand as they went up the stairs and into the front door. Shutting it behind him, he pulled Meg back into his arms and kissed her. Meg relaxed against him and kissed him back. His lips were soft and gentle, full of longing. When he finally pulled away, he didn't release her.

"I have missed you so much." His voice was soft, only for her to hear. His finger traced down her cheek to her chin and then touched her lips again. His eyes lingered on her lips. For a moment, Meg thought, no hoped, he was going to kiss her again.

"Meg, is that you?" a voice called from the kitchen. Gran was up.

Meg stayed snuggled close to Jack. "I've missed you, too. I'm so glad you're here."

His lips brushed hers one more time before he released her. "We better go see Gran," he said with a grin.

"Yes, Gran. It's me," Meg called back. "I have a surprise for you."

Gran laughed and clapped her hands, then hugged her "dear boy" when Jack followed Meg into the kitchen. Then she had to hear all about his trip and find out if he'd had anything to eat. For a few minutes, everything seemed normal. Meg forgot all about the fact that Gran was dying.

Chapter Thirty-seven

Jack's arrival brought Gran renewed energy. That afternoon, they finished half of the apples Meg had kept. The next day they did the rest. Jack pitched in to help, operating the apple peeler as though he'd been doing it his whole life. They emptied the pots and filled the canning jars again and again all day. As they sat talking in the living room that evening, the occasional musical sound of the jars sealing rang down the hallway.

"What are you going to do?" Jack asked the next afternoon as the two of them sat on the porch swing, his arm draped behind Meg's back, her head resting on his shoulder. Gran slept in her room, the busy events of the last two days having caught up with her at last.

"I don't know. I didn't see how bad she was until after the Independence Day celebration. Uncle Daniel came several times to check her. He said she was fine, that maybe she had a summer cold and it would go away. Then we got busy with the summer canning and I didn't pay as much attention to how she was feeling. She never complained. She just got slower." Meg shook her head. "It worried me to leave her before, but now I don't know what to do."

"We'll wait a little longer to get married," Jack suggested and squeezed Meg's shoulder.

"No. I want Gran to be there when I get married. It's her dream, too. The only trouble is that I don't know if I can leave her right away after we're married."

"The harvesting is well in hand. Dad and Steven can handle it. Steve didn't go to college this semester because he wanted to earn money to pay for it before he went. He'll leave in January, but Dad will be able to manage on his own at that time of year. We can stay here and take care of Gran for a while, if you'd like," Jack said.

"If you don't mind, I'd like that very much." Meg had never felt so relieved.

"It's settled then. I'll send a telegram to my parents for them to come for a wedding next week. They were waiting on me to tell them when to come. We can get married, as we planned, and then stay here for a while and see how things go." Jack grinned, wrapped both arms around her, and squeezed her. "Just think. Next week we'll be married!"

∞

The week was a whirlwind. Uncle Daniel and Aunt Elaine returned from Boston. Jack's parents and sister arrived. Jack had gotten his height from his father, but his looks from his mother. She was a petite woman with the same sandy blonde hair and hazel eyes. Jack's father adored her. Jack's sister, Adele, was the image of her mother, except her fine, straight hair had been cut into a bob. Meg adored her immediately.

The morning of their wedding day dawned clear and bright. Even though it was quite cool, the sunshine promised a warm afternoon. The simple meal they would eat after the wedding was sitting in the icebox, ready to heat and set out when the ceremony was finished. Gran had insisted on making an apple cake. The effort had tired her out, but she was proud of it.

Meg dressed in her room. Adele came to help her with her hair and promised to stand up with her at the wedding. Meg wished Nellie was there, too.

Meg thought back to a time, almost exactly a year ago, when she had walked into a hospital room and found a soldier in excruciating pain. The man she would marry today had walked through that and come out victorious. She imagined him at the hospital ball, struggling

207

through basic dance steps. She thought of the day he'd gone sledding with them, or swimming in the ocean.

Uncertainty lay before them. Gran grew weaker every day, though she was fighting for all she was worth. Meg didn't know how long they would stay here, but the fact that Jack was willing to love her and stay here with her until Gran no longer needed her filled her heart with joy and relief.

Uncle Daniel drove them to the church later that morning. Gran and Aunt Elaine went in while Uncle Daniel waited to give her away. The doors opened. Meg saw a tall, strong, sandy-haired man standing in the front of the church in full dress uniform. A broad grin spread across his face as he watched them enter and walk down the aisle.

Meg had never looked more beautiful. Jack watched her walk down the aisle on her uncle's arm. Her hair had been pinned up, but a wisp had come loose and drifted across her cheek. Her soft cheek. In a few minutes, their long wait would be over. He could hardly wait to call her his wife. Meg and her uncle stopped in front of Pastor Norton. Uncle Daniel took Meg's hand from the crook of his arm and held it out to Jack.

"You look so beautiful," Jack whispered as he stepped closer and took her hand for the ceremony. "You're the most beautiful bride I've ever seen. And you're mine."

Meg flushed and smiled up at him from under her lashes. Then they turned to face the pastor.

The service was over so quickly. As hard as Meg tried to remember every moment, she felt like she'd forgotten half of it before it was over.

Everyone was there – Dr. and Mrs. Grey, Nurse Rogers, Dr and Mrs. Fulton, Mr. and Mrs. Miller, the Stuart family, and about half of the church. After the simple ceremony and once they'd greeted everyone, Jack and Meg walked back to Gran's house, enjoying the time alone before the big lunch with everyone. Jack tucked Meg's hand into the crook of his arm.

Meg clung to him, leaning her head against his shoulder. "Remember when you needed a cane to get around town?"

"Remember when I was sure I'd never walk again?"

"You needed someone to encourage you that you *could*."

"God sent you to me that day in the hospital. I was so low, so discouraged. But you came along and told me I could do it, so I did."

"And here we are." They'd reached Gran's road. Several autos were already parked outside. Meg faced her husband. "Are you sure you don't mind living here for a while?"

"As long as I can be with you, I'll happily live anywhere. But Meg, I don't think it will be long." Jack caught Meg's chin and lifted it until she met his eyes. "I'm here, with you, through everything that happens in the next few weeks."

Meg nodded, too choked up to speak. Jack brushed away the lone tear that slid down her cheek. Swallowing hard, Meg was finally able to whisper, "I'm blissfully happy today. We've been dreaming of this day for so long. At the same time, I see Gran and how frail she's become and it's bittersweet. It's this cloud hanging over the happiness."

"It's a tiny cloud, barely anything to consider. I've never seen Gran as happy as she was today. So you remind yourself of that every day, my darling girl. Ready for what comes next?"

Meg nodded. They walked down the road to Gran's house and their wedding lunch.

Chapter Thirty-eight

Gran failed rapidly after that. Even though she could barely move around without getting winded, she still rose before Meg and Jack and started the coffee. Meg would hurry downstairs to help Gran to her easy chair where she could enjoy it by the front window.

One morning in November, Meg woke to a silent house. She heard no noise at all from Gran. The eastern sky was stained a deep pink when Meg dove out of bed and rushed downstairs, tying her bathrobe around her as she went. She found Gran in bed, her breathing shallow, labored.

"Gran?" she whispered. "Do you need anything?"

"I'm sorry, dearie. I can't seem to get out of bed to start the coffee."

"Oh, Gran, you never needed to do that. I'm happy to make it. Do you want me to bring you a cup? Do you want to move to your seat in the living room?" Meg was fighting tears at the sight of Gran's helpless form.

"I think I'll rest here for a bit. Get my strength up. Could you help me with another pillow? I'm having trouble catching my breath."

Jack appeared, fully dressed, in the doorway and motioned that he was going for the doctor. Meg nodded and returned her attention to her Gran.

"Is that dear boy going for Dr. Grey? Tell him the doctor can't do anything for me anymore."

Meg shifted a pillow behind Gran's shoulders and neck and tucked another behind it so she was propped up. "Dr. Grey might be able to make you more comfortable. Besides, I'll feel better if he comes and checks you. Is that better?"

Gran nodded. "I can breathe a little better."

"I'm going to start the stove and stir the fire in the living room. I'll be right back to check on you."

"Take your time, dearie. I don't feel like going anywhere." Gran's eyes slid shut as she dozed off.

∞

A grim-faced Dr. Grey exited Gran's room. Meg was waiting for him, pacing the hall outside her room.

"She's asleep," he said.

"Do you want a cup of coffee?" Meg asked.

"That would be nice," Dr. Grey answered and followed Meg to the kitchen.

Jack had taken a delivery job at the Hollis Hardware store and would be home for lunch in another hour. The smell of the food filled the air.

"Would you like a something to eat?" Meg offered as she poured a cup of coffee and set it in front of the doctor.

"As delicious as it smells, my wife is expecting me for lunch. Thank you for the offer, though." He sipped the coffee, then stared into the cup. Meg waited expectantly on the other side of the small table.

"Your Gran doesn't have much longer to live." Dr. Grey finally raised his eyes to meet Meg's. "Fluid is building up around her heart and lungs and her body can't get rid of it. The best we can do is make her comfortable. I wish I had better news." He reached across the table to squeeze Meg's folded hands. "I'll be by to check on her every day. Will you and Jack be able to take care of her?"

"That's why we stayed. I can't imagine being anywhere else right now."

"It will be normal for her to sleep a lot. She might struggle with confusion. But she probably won't experience much pain. If she does, I'll see what I can do to alleviate it. You might want to get in touch with your Aunt Elaine so she can say goodbye."

Meg nodded, unable to speak around the tightness in her throat.

"Yes. Well." Dr. Grey sniffed loudly and wiped his own nose with his handkerchief. He stood to leave. "I'll be by tomorrow unless you need me sooner."

Meg saw him to the door. She held on to her emotions until it was shut behind him. Then she sank, sobbing, onto the floor. Jack found her there when he came home for lunch a few minutes later. He gathered his wife into his arms and let her cry onto him until all her tears were spent.

Aunt Elaine arrived the next day. She slept on the couch in the living room so she could be nearby. After that, Gran failed before their eyes. They took turns sitting with her, only leaving her alone for short periods at a time.

One night, early in December, Meg jerked awake and listened to the sounds around her. She could hear Jack snoring in the bedroom above her. She heard Aunt Elaine shift on the couch. She probably wasn't sleeping, either. It took Meg a moment to determine what was different.

Then it came to her. She could no longer hear the labored sound of Gran's breathing.

Her fingers fumbled with a match as she tried to light a lantern. Once the light streamed across the bed, Meg saw it. Gran's face, as peaceful in death as it had been in life, held a little smile, like she knew a secret she'd never tell anyone.

Aunt Elaine appeared in the doorway. "What's happened?" she whispered. Her gaze fell on Gran. She stumbled across the room and dropped to her knees by Gran's bed. Her fingers gently stroked the old woman's soft hand.

"What do we do now?" Meg asked.

"We live our life and enjoy every day, just like she did. Just like she would want us to do." Aunt Elaine turned a tear streaked face toward Meg. "But it's going to be so hard to do it without her, isn't it?"

∞

The next difficult weeks were spent in saying goodbye to Gran and Hollis. Aunt Elaine helped Meg pack a few keepsakes she knew Gran would have wanted her to take with her into a trunk they found in the attic. Little by little, they prepared the house so it could be closed up until Aunt Elaine could decide what to do with it. Jack bought train tickets to Indiana.

Dr. Grey took them to the station on the day of their departure. Meg hugged him with all her might. Jack shook hands. They boarded the train. Meg stared out the window at Walton until she could no longer see it.

"Do you regret leaving?" Jack asked. Meg could hear the nerves in his voice.

"No. No regrets. But that doesn't mean I won't miss it." Meg sniffed and wiped her face with her handkerchief.

"I understand exactly what you mean," Jack said. He wrapped his arms around his wife and drew her close as they traveled west.

Two days later, Meg stepped off of a train in Indiana. Jack still hadn't told her his secret.

The ride down the long country road offered a good chance for Jack to tell Meg about his community. He had a story about each house as they passed in the farm truck his father had left at the station the previous evening. The lane for his family's farm approached on their left. They could see the house and out buildings from the road.

"I can hardly wait for you to see all this in the summer when everything is green and growing," Jack said as he waved his hand around at their surroundings. He continued past the lane and on down the road.

Meg looked puzzled. "I thought you said your parents are expecting us to come for supper."

"They are. But there's something I wanted to show you first." Jack kept his eyes facing front and face serious. Meg could see a familiar twinkle in his eye that told her he was up to something.

They rounded a bend in the road and continued across a wooden bridge. Another lane turned off to the left. Jack followed it. A row of poplars lined the drive on each side. At the end of the lane stood a small, white house, the porch on the front complete with a swing. A tiny gable poked out over the top of the porch and another at the end of the house.

Jack pulled the truck to a stop in front of the house and motioned for Meg to wait for a moment. He got out and unlocked the house. Then, he came back for Meg. He opened her door and handed her out. Keeping hold of her hand, he led her up to the house.

"Welcome home," Jack spoke close to her ear. Without warning, he swept her up into his arms and carried her over the threshold. Setting her back onto the floor, he kissed his wife.

Meg wrapped her arms around his neck and kissed him back. "You kept your promise," she murmured against his lips.

"I always keep my promises," Jack murmured back, "including my promise to love you forever."

Author's Note

In 2008, the H1N1 virus was running rampant through the state of Texas. We were living in Bowie at the time, attending a linguistics school in preparation for moving to Uganda, Africa as missionaries. One of the other missionary families brought the virus to our school and it marched its way through our number. Our entire family was sick almost at once. I don't remember ever having been that sick in my entire life. It took us over a month to get completely better because of secondary infections we all developed after being sick.

During that time, I researched this particular virus. I didn't want us to have a cytokine storm, the primary cause for the majority of the deaths during the 1918 Spanish Flu epidemic. My research into boosting our immune systems without making them attack healthy cells led to research into the Spanish Flu epidemic and then into World War 1.

In 2011, we were living in Uganda. A friend had introduced me to the National Novel Writing Month Young Writer's Program. I wanted to teach my children creative writing. Their program was free and well done. Meanwhile, I decided that if my children were going to do it, I should participate with them. I thought back to my research a few years earlier and decided to write a story that took place at the end of the Great War, during the Spanish Flu epidemic. Thus, Promising Meg was born in its original form, One Winter. It was the first time I completed a novel of over 50,000 words in my life.

The book has been through multiple (much needed!) revisions as I learned the art over the last few years. I'm thankful I can tell you it's much improved over its original version.

Acknowledgements

Thank you so much to my husband, James, to Rachel Miller, my sister Joanna, Christine Campbell, and Sandy Panagos for reading this book when it was terrible. And I mean terrible. Embarrassingly awful. More importantly, thanks for looking for positives when you read it. Thank you, James, for not adding ninjas. They might make most things better, but I'm pretty sure they don't improve romance novels. I'll keep them in mind for later writing projects. <3

Thank you to my beta readers, Rachel Miller (bless you, you were brave enough to read it twice!), Kris Loomis, and Judy Sutton. Your suggestions were invaluable and I took every one of them to heart.

Thank you to every one of my ARC readers. You guys are a huge help getting this book out there, into the wild, where people can read and enjoy it.

Thanks to the Create If group and our fearless leader, Kirsten. You all inspire me to try things I wouldn't otherwise attempt.

Finally, I'm so thankful to God for giving us, not just what we need to get by, but wonderful, creative talents that help us thrive in this beautiful world He created.

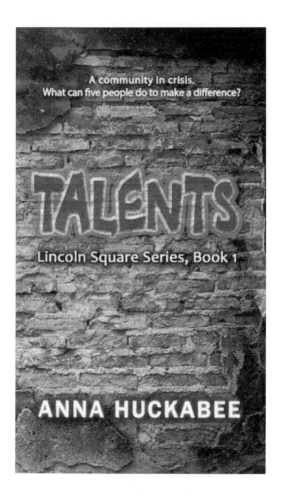

A community in crisis.
What can five people do to make a difference?

TALENTS

Lincoln Square Series, Book 1

ANNA HUCKABEE

Look for other books by Anna Huckabee on www.amazon.com/Anna-Huckabee including her Lincoln Square series.

Follow Anna on her blog: www.annahuckabee.com and sign up for her email update to stay apprised of any future releases.

Made in the USA
Columbia, SC
19 June 2019